FALLING FOR HIS BEST FRIEND'S SISTER

THE GREAT LOVELY FALLS - BOOK TWO

ALIE GARNETT

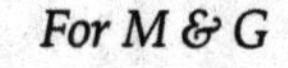

For M & G

MEET THE LOVELY'S

Sera Lovely –35-year-old who is the Director of HR, mom of 2, step-mom to 5, engaged to Harrison Dean

Harper Lovely - 30-year-old who is CEO/CFO/just plain C of Lovely Catering with Lucy and Boss of all those around her.

Mabel Lucie Atwell Lovely - 28-year-old who is Lucy's twin and Children's Lit professor at the U. And is sick and tired of her twin shenanigans.

Lucy Lovely - 28-year-old who is a twin to Mabel, Works for Lovely catering and cleans offices. Best friend to Cliff Scott.

Agatha Lovely - 26-year-old who is an amazing artist and mediocre bartender looking for a job (if you know of one tell her)

Buzz Lovely – 25-year-old reporter for the times, youngest and more outgoing of the big girls (Psst: if you have a lead on a good story, Buzz needs a break)

Emmaline Lovely – 15-year-old sullen teen who pretends not to care about her family.

Violet Lovely – 8-year-old upbeat, outgoing artist.

CHAPTER ONE

"Ms. Lovely," Kirk Langley said in his slightly high-pitched voice from behind her, causing the hair on Mabel's arms to rise. She stifled a shiver. The way he said her name always made her think that he was calling her pretty and not just using her last name. Mabel Lucie Lovely, to be exact. Kirk had been her mentor since she had started teaching at the U two years before, and she hadn't gotten used to him yet.

In that time, he hadn't hidden the fact that he was interested in being more than her mentor, or mentor in other ways, as he had even said once. Gross.

Mabel tried not to let his advances get to her; she was within a year of getting her doctorate, and then she wouldn't be under him anymore. Another gross image.

"Hello, Kirk," she said, not turning her chair toward him in the doorway of her tiny office. Hoping that if he thought she was busy, he would leave quicker. Her office was on the fourth floor of the English building, and despite its size, she liked it because it was warm a lot of the year. Mabel didn't do cold, ever.

"You look beautiful today, Lucie," his words sent a chill down her spine. Nobody called her by her middle name. Or maybe the instant chill was caused by his hand touched her shoulders and slid down the front of her blouse that was not as thick as she would have liked it to be right now. No material was that thick.

Pushing his hands away, she jumped out of her chair and away from him in the small space. "What the hell are you doing, Kirk?" she hissed.

For his part, Kirk looked sad that she had rejected him.

"I just thought we had a connection." He didn't hide the fact that he was looking at her chest, not her face. That might have been because his eye level was closer to her chest than her eyes, but she was sure that wasn't the reason.

"What? Why?" she stammered. There was never a connection at all. That was all in his head. When she had first started teaching, he had taken her out for supper. She had thought it was a nice gesture from a new colleague, but he had assumed that they were dating. Or more than dating. It had been hard to put him in him his place two years ago, and now, for some reason, she would have to do it again.

"Friday night? Remember?" His pale watery brown eyes pleaded with her to remember.

She did not. She had been home with her little sisters watching something on TV with a cartoon princess. Her fifteen-year-old sister Emma still loved the cartoons as much as eight-year-old Violet did. Mabel, not so much, but it was date night for her stepmom and her fiancé, so Mabel had agreed to stay home with them. Not that she had a life anyway, and on top of that, babysitting got her out of helping her sisters' catering business. Princesses won out over waitressing any day.

"I'm sorry, Kirk, I don't." She shrugged, trying to figure out exactly what could have happened.

"The fundraiser. You said you weren't going, but you did." He kicked at the green carpet on her floor.

Mabel could only think of one fundraiser: an event for the basketball team, something she would never in a million years have attended. She was not into sports and didn't have the money to donate anyway. She was still paying on her student loans and living at home.

But the reminder was enough to make her realize exactly what had happened. The pieces of the puzzle all fell into place. The fundraiser had been a catered event. One guess as to who had done the catering.

Fuck, she wanted to yell through the hallways. *Fuck you, Lucy!* Not that her sister would hear her, she was still sleeping in her bed at home, most likely with the skanky on-and-off boyfriend who had obviously been off on Friday night. But Mabel had seen Kevin sneaking out of the house on Sunday morning, so they must be back on again.

"I think you're mistaken, Kirk. I was home with my sisters." She didn't add that he had seen her sister. Lucy Maud was her identical twin. Mabel loved the girl, but sometimes she did shitty things.

"No, no, Lucie. It was you," he argued. The repeated use of the name "Lucie" was enough to convince her she was right about who he had been with on Friday.

"I can have my mom call you. She knows I was at home. We had pizza and ice cream," she tried, maybe he would forget her.

"Maybe you were on drugs or drunk," Kirk said hopefully.

Mabel was sure it would take more than using both at the same time to get her to look twice at Kirk. Beyond the creepy part of him, there was the fact that he was uncomfortable in his own skin. It surprised her that Lucy would give him a second look, or even a first one. He wasn't her type. Well, he was nobody's type.

"No. My name is Mabel. Says so on the door." She pointed to the placard behind him.

"Mabel Lucie." He stated, and she cursed her parents for saddling her with two first names.

"But it was not me. You know everyone has someone who looks like them out there." Another angle, maybe this one would land.

"Sister?" he asked, but Mabel was not admitting to that because then he would want to date her sister. And Mabel didn't need him in her life as anything, even her sister's boyfriend. Not to mention he couldn't handle Lucy. As the family's wild child, she was a handful. Kirk, in no way, was up for *that* challenge.

"Why would anyone name one kid Mabel Lucie and the other Lucy?" Well, her parents had because they were nuts. Or maybe just one of them. She hadn't seen either since she had been thirteen, so she couldn't tell you which was to blame. So, she blamed them both.

"You're right. Wow, she looked just like you. When I called her Mabel Lucie, she corrected me and said, 'just Lucie,'" he struggled, finally accepting it hadn't been her at all. Though his eyes creepily caressed her breasts again.

"Crazy," she agreed, relieved he finally had given up. "I have to run and get something from the cafeteria."

She started to gather up her purse and school bag as he continued to stare at her like a creep. Turning with her stuff, he finally smiled and stepped back to let her pass.

"Okay," he said, following her as she left the office.

"See you later then." Mabel turned down the hallway and hurried to the stairway. After going down half a dozen steps, she turned and watched with relief as he went the other direction towards his own office. Standing stock-still on the stairs, she listened to his footsteps until she heard the door to his office close. She could finally breathe again.

Once she was sure he wasn't coming back, Mabel climbed back up the stairs, hurried into her office, and shut the door. Leaning against it, she tried to get her anger under control but failed. This was the worst thing her twin had done in years, and Lucy had done some shit lately.

Pulling her phone from her pocket, she found the contact she wanted and waited as the phone rang. The phone rang until her voice-mail kicked in with Lucy's singing an old Reba McIntire song about nobody calling. Mabel hung up without leaving a message and called again. And again.

Pulling away from the door, she threw herself into her office chair and dialed different numbers until she finally got an answer.

"What, Maby?" Her sister Agatha sounded pissed and tired, though not pissed enough to call her anything but her nickname. But then again, Agatha had only probably been asleep for a few hours. As an artist and a bartender, her days began in the afternoon and ended as the sun came up.

"Get out of bed and get Lucy fucking Maud on the phone," Mabel calmly said.

"Why? I'm not getting up for nothing," Agatha replied. Mabel had thought her sister would say that. Agatha was predictable.

"She fucked my boss," Mabel hissed the words quietly in the phone because she was still at work. Words she hoped to god weren't true.

"I'm heading down and putting this shit on speaker phone." Agatha was suddenly awake and chipper. It was the little things that got her sister going.

"No," Mabel said about speakerphone but was sure Agatha would do whatever she wanted to.

"Oh, yeah, and I'm not knocking." Mabel heard the sound of a door opening and Agatha saying loudly, "Lucy, time to get up. Maby wants to talk to you." Sometimes it was hard to believe that all three women were past the age of twenty-five and still acted this way. Hell, the twins were closer to thirty than twenty-five. But then again, maturity happened slowly in the Lovely house.

"Kevin, you might want to leave for this one. Nice dick." Mabel heard Agatha say loudly to the loser in her sister's bed. Then speaking directly to Mabel, she said into the phone, "It's not, actually. Nothing to write home about. I have seen smaller, but not often and not when it was important."

Mabel hated hearing that man was even with her sister, but she wasn't surprised. The man was a cheat and wasn't smart enough to try and hide the fact. Lucy was easy to forgive and forget, always taking him back.

Chuckling at Agatha's description, Mabel wondered when she had seen a penis that wasn't important. She heard a thump and a rustle of blankets.

"What is the matter with you, Maby?" Lucy said into Agatha's phone.

"You fucked my boss, Lucy Maud Montgomery Lovely." Maby

wasted no time and decided that the use of her sister's entire name was warranted. Each of her sisters had been named in honor of an author, except Maby herself, who was named for an illustrator of children's books. Coupled with their unusual last name, the use of their full names was always annoying. But when it was needed, it was needed.

"I did not, Mabel Lucie Attwell Lovely." Lucy defended herself, pulling out the big one herself.

"Kirk Langley? Ring any bells? Did he ring your bell?"

"No, he tried, but no. He was like stalker material. I danced with him once because I felt sorry for him, and he kept asking. And then he followed me around the rest of the night while I was working."

"Were you drinking?" Mabel questioned. Just because Lucy was working didn't mean she was completely sober.

"Yes, Harper was being a bitch," Lucy said of their older sister, who was the actual brains behind the catering business that Lucy and Harper ran. For three years, they had been trying to make a go of their company, and it was finally taking off.

"Do you even remember? He seems to think you went all the way," Maby answered as if they were back in high school.

"Ask him."

"I am not asking him! You were there. He thinks I fucked him."

"Ohhh, Maby had sex," Lucy said into the phone.

"Do you have sex, Maby?" Agatha's voice filled the line. She must have grabbed the phone back. Recently, the running joke in the Lovely house was that Mabel hadn't had sex yet.

"I have had sex many times, but not with my boss."

"You should. Your boss might be just what you need to loosen you up," Agatha stated.

"No, she shouldn't!" Lucy yelled. Agatha must still be holding it.

"Gross," Mabel said and hung up on them since her sister wasn't going to actually tell her what she wanted to know. Probably because she had slept with him. It wouldn't be the first time Lucy had lied; Mabel just had to figure out why she was lying.

Her sisters drove her nuts, all of them. Except the youngest two—

they were great, but Emma was fifteen now and on the cusp of turning into a teenager. That was when the Lovely sisters seemed to let their wild sides take over. Their stepmom hadn't even tried to control them.

That might be why all the sisters were sometimes a bit out of control; Sera had made them that way. But Mabel wouldn't trade Sera for any mother in the world, and that included her own biological mom. Sera had married the girls' dad when the twins were thirteen. Harper had been fifteen, and the Agatha and Bea had been eleven and ten. Looking back, Mabel would never have been able to do what Sera had done, taking on all those kids. At the time, Sera had only been nineteen and pregnant, and the father hadn't been Mabel's dad either.

By the time Sera's baby had been born, the girls' dad was long gone, and Sera had found herself raising six girls alone and not even able to enjoy alcohol legally. But she did it, and she kept doing it until each and every one had turned eighteen—and long after. Few of Mabel's sisters had left home, and those that had, had returned.

Recently Sera had met the man of her dreams and was supposed to finally move out, taking the two little ones with her. So far, that hadn't happened. Every time it was brought up, there had been a new excuse. Not that Sera wasn't in love with Harrison; it was just that she secretly wanted him to move in. Harrison wasn't having it.

Mabel knew it was going to take an intervention to actually get her out of the house, but so far, Harrison only had a two-bedroom condo and not enough room for three more. They had been looking for the perfect house, but Sera hadn't found anything she liked. Until she did, there was no getting her out of the Lovely house.

Slipping the phone back into her pocket, Mabel once again decided that she hated that her parents had given their children the same names. Sure, they were twins, but it didn't mean they needed to share the same name. Mabel grudgingly conceded that their names weren't *exactly* the same. Lucy had been lucky enough to be named after a famous author of children's literature, whereas Mabel was named after a children's book illustrator that nobody had ever heard of. Thus, always making the *What's your middle name?* question a lesson in art history.

The twins weren't the only ones saddled with odd names. Their oldest sister, Nelle Harper Lee, had always seemed the winner in Mabel's mind at Lovely names. Agatha Christie had lost big time, which might be why she was always hiding in her room. Beatrix Potter Lovely seemed to come in second and embraced her name completely, going by Buzz with the family and Bea to her friends.

Since the youngest two, Emma and Violet, didn't share the same biological parents as the older five girls, they were blessed and didn't hate their names.

Mabel sat down at her desk. Maybe no one had seen what had happened at the benefit on Friday. She and her twin did look a little different after twenty-eight years. Surely, they looked different after all that time.

CHAPTER TWO

By midday, Mabel hadn't forgiven her sister. In fact, she was madder than ever, except now she was hiding in her office from not only her boss but all her coworkers also. Since morning the office gossip mill had been hard at work, and everyone knew what had happened, and nobody believed that it had been her sister who had been with Kirk. Yes, Mabel had finally thrown Lucy under the bus, but it didn't matter. Most thought that she had made the twin thing up.

Tossing a few books in her bag, she headed out after sending an email to Kirk that she was taking the rest of the week off, not even caring that it was only Monday. This was definitely going to take a week to die down, and there was no way she was coming back to the office before that happened. Good thing the semester hadn't started yet.

Mabel locked her office with the hope that it really would only take a week for the rumors to die down. The drive home was quick, and she was inside and tossing anything from clothes to her precious makeup from her sister's room into the hallway in no time. Yes, it was childish, but it felt so good, and Lucy deserved everything she got.

Mabel considered the pile in the hallway. Were they even close anymore? When was the last time she had done something even close to this to her twin? Should she put it all back and just talk to her, believe her denials? They needed to start acting like adults.

"Are we throwing it on the lawn or just leaving it here in a pile?" Agatha asked, her hands braced on the doorframe. The noise must have woken her up, though Agatha didn't look like she had been asleep.

Mabel dismissed the adulting idea and kicked at the pile. "If you're willing to help, the lawn." Suddenly, seeing all of Lucy's possessions on the lawn was a priority.

"Always willing to fuck off a sister." Agatha grabbed the green comforter and balled-up sheets and dragged them toward the stairs.

"You're the best, Ag!" Mabel yelled as her sister grabbed a pile of clothes that had been further down the hallway and added it to her load.

Once the bedding and all of Lucy's clothes, including her bras and panties, were strewn across the green grass of the front yard (and maybe some in the neighbor's lawn and fence), Mabel was a little happier. Not happy enough to forgive, but happy enough to not be completely pissed at Lucy.

Mabel went back upstairs to find anything she had missed and found Agatha laid out on the bare mattress, wearing a sweatshirt despite the heat of the day and the work they had just done. Wiping sweat from her brow, Agatha asked, "Did you hide her plane ticket?"

Spinning to her sister, she said, "What plane ticket?"

"Lucy, Cliff, and those jokers they hang with are going to Florida this evening. She can't go if she doesn't have a ticket. Next time she'll think before she fucks your boss." Agatha didn't move from the bed but rolled over and pulled open the nightstand drawer—something that Mabel had missed while cleaning out the room. Agatha pulled a piece of paper from the drawer and waved it around in the air.

Grabbing it, Mabel read the name printed on the ticket: Lucy M. Lovely. The flight was leaving today and would return long before she needed to be back at work. "No way am I hiding this. I am taking a fucking vacation."

It would not only get her out of the house but away from her twin for a few days. By Monday, Kirk would have forgotten anything that might or might not have happened.

Agatha sat up, grinning. "Do you think it'll work? How are you going to sneak on the plane?"

"I don't have to. Her purse is right here." She closed the closet door, revealing the oversized red bag. Her driver's license would be in there. There were some advantages to being identical twins.

Mabel looked at the tickets again. She should feel a little guilty about even attempting this. And if Lucy showed before the plane left in five hours, she would hand over the ticket and apologize. If she didn't show up, Mabel would pay her back for the ticket and even work as a cater-waiter for her for a month. Until then, she had to pack for a trip. Spinning on her heels, she headed down the hallway to her own bedroom.

Agatha rolled off the bed and followed, asking, "Won't her merry group of misfits notice you?"

"Who's going?" Mabel asked.

"Cliff and I'm sure pencil-dick Kevin, and that Beth who can't keep her pants on," Agatha said. For all her pretending to not care, Agatha always knew what was going on in the house.

"I can fool them until we get there, then I'll ditch them when we arrive. They'll probably be fucking their way across the peninsula anyway. I'm not concerned." She wondered if she truly was up for the challenge. It had been years since she had pretended to be her twin, but it would be worth it for a free vacation.

"Kevin was in her bed this morning," Agatha pointed out as she fell onto Mabel's bed and looked at the ceiling. "What if he wants to join the mile-high club?"

"Gross. If it comes to that, I'll just break up with him for her. Again. She deserves better than him … as long as it's not my boss." Mabel opened her closet to see what she had that was vacation appropriate.

"What if Cliff does?" Agatha wiggled a brow at her.

"That's just as bad as Kevin, only I think he has an easier time getting laid," she said of Lucy's bestie. Cliff couldn't keep it in his pants any more than her sister. Odd that he and Lucy had never hooked up, but maybe they had, and Mabel didn't know. The few times she'd met him, she hadn't been unimpressed.

With Cliff, she was certain she could bluff her way, though. Mabel knew how to act like her twin. In high school, they had switched places many times and had never been caught. This would be no different. No way were Lucy and Cliff close enough that she couldn't fool him. Mabel was certain Beth wouldn't figure it out either. Fooling Kevin would be her biggest challenge because Mabel refused to touch that man, ever. Even for a free vacation.

CHAPTER THREE

WALKING INTO THE TERMINAL, the first thing Cliff Scott saw was Lucy Lovely sitting, waiting for him with her head down, looking at her phone. He couldn't believe Lucy was already there. Lucy hadn't been early for anything since he had met her almost a year before. But here she was in a gray V-neck T-shirt that said Cancun on it. Or actually, it said "Cancan" because Lucy couldn't spell. All her shirts featured some type of mistake she had made while she had a screen-printing business that went belly up a few years before. Though she hated them and what they represented, she still wore them. He loved them and liked that she was willingly wearing her failures on her chest, unapologetic.

"Luce, are Kevin and Beth here yet?" he called to her as soon as he was close enough, so he wasn't yelling.

"Nope," was all she said, not even bothering to look at him. Cliff was taken aback. This was not a typical Lucy response. Her enthusiasm for life always trickled into everything she said and did. It's what drew him in from the beginning.

"Are you hungover?" Maybe that was the explanation. The only time Lucy wasn't upbeat was when she was hungover.

"A little," she admitted, not looking up at him and not smiling at the question. She put her phone away and tapping her fingers on her leg in the usual Lucy fashion. Lucy hadn't stopped moving since he first met her; something was always twitching.

"You seem like it. I can't believe you're not more excited. St. Pete Beach, baby." He grinned at her. Lucy was one of his best friends, but today she was grouchy. Yesterday, she was nothing but chatty and exciting about the trip. Maybe because she and Kevin were off again, and Cliff hated Kevin. He was a toad.

"St. Pete Beach!" Lucy yelled so loud that people stopped and looked at her, but she didn't care. That's what he loved about her.

"No kidding, baby. Do you think those two are going to skip it?" Cliff plopped down next to her and threw his arm around her. The other couple had only been dating for a few weeks. When the trip had been planned, Kevin had been dating Lucy, and Cliff had been dating Beth. That had blown when Kevin had cheated on Lucy with Beth. Lucy was taking her break-up with Kevin hard and wasn't over it yet. With their past, Cliff wasn't sure she wouldn't take him back, given half a chance.

Now weeks later, they were all going on vacation together because the tickets were already purchased, and the other couple couldn't understand what Cliff and Lucy's problem was. Being together didn't make them smarter.

Over a year ago, he had met Lucy Lovely in a bar. She had been dancing on the bar, and he had caught her when she fell off. It sounded romantic, but he had none of those feelings for her. Not at all. Maybe because when they met, she had been dating a guy they both actually knew. Or maybe because he would rather have Lucy as a friend than only as a one-night stand. And Cliff was not looking for anything other than a one-night stand.

"They would be nuts to miss this trip." She leaned forward to put her phone in her bag at her feet.

"No kidding, right?" he said, running his fingers lightly down her back over the tight material of the shirt as she bent over. He had done this a hundred times over the last year, but this time, her skin gave off little shots of electricity as he went. Cliff resisted the temptation to do it again.

She straightened up and looked at him with her brown eyes, like she had felt the spark too. Ignoring it, Cliff pulled his arm away and leaned down to pull a box from his bag and tossed it onto her lap.

"What's this?" she demanded, not touching the box.

"I hope you know what condoms are, Luce. I owe you, remember? I passed out before you did last weekend, so I owe you a full box. Notice I got you the small ones because I know how you like your men." He grinned at her, proud of his joke. "And this way, I'll never have to borrow from you since they don't fit my extra-large dick."

"Oh, please," she exclaimed and laughed. "You're just giving them to me because they were too big for you. Small doesn't always mean small *enough*."

"Do you need me to show you right now how wrong you are?" He pulled on her dark brown ponytail, glad that she was already pulling out of her funk.

"No! There are kids around. I'd hate for them to start having nightmares because of you." She held up the box and then bent to put it in her bag.

At the sight of the gap between the waistband of her shorts and her shirt, Cliff was unable to stop himself from running the palm of his hand up her bare back. Again, her body gave off little shocks as he touched it, so faint but unmistakable.

Sitting up, she trapped his hand between her body and the chair, pressing hard. "You will not snap my bra in the airport."

"I was doing no such thing." Laughing, he tried to tug his hand back, but she did not reduce the pressure.

"Bull. You were," she accused and squashed his hand more into the chair.

"I am now." He tried to pull his hand out again and failed, so he flexed his fingers to show he wasn't completely trapped by her, that he could still touch her.

"You're lying to me, Cliff," she still sounded mad, but she was holding back a grin. That is until her body instantly went stiff.

Looking away from her, he saw Kevin and Beth walk into the waiting area. "Fuck. I can't believe they actually showed up."

Her head swiveled around, looking for who he was talking about, but she couldn't seem to pin them down. Odd, since she had known Kevin and Beth longer than him.

Kevin sauntered up to them and grinned when he saw Cliff's hand on Lucy's back. "So, you two are hooking up? Nice."

"We are not," Lucy hissed, looking closely at Kevin.

"She's lying to you, Kev. We've been fucking for days, weeks even." Cliff leaned over and kissed her cheek, hoping she would play along. The cheater deserved the turnaround.

"Oh. I had forgotten," she said, not very convincing.

"You're forgettable, Cliff." Kevin laughed as Beth walked up behind him and slid her arms around him, showing possession of the man who didn't deserve his best friend. Cliff had never thought Kevin was good enough for Lucy from the beginning.

"Not as forgettable as you are … Kyle? Is that your name?"

"Funny, Lucy. You won't easily forget this dick." He ran his hand over his crotch as if his new girlfriend wasn't hanging on his back. If he had been smart, her instant scowl should have made the man stop, but he *was* Kevin.

"Is that the same dick that my sister called 'nothing to write home about' this morning? And why were you in bed with me this morning, Kevin?"

Cliff looked at her in shock as his hand slid from its confinement. Why had Kevin been in her bed this morning? What had happened the night before? He had been bartending, and she had been hanging out at the bar. He thought she'd gone home alone.

"Kevin?" Beth questioned from behind him. Her shock matched Cliff's.

"We didn't do anything, Beth. Her place was closer to the bar." Kevin backed slowly away from Cliff and Lucy as he tried to explain away the morning.

"My sister saw his dick, Beth. I wouldn't put too much stock in his innocence," Lucy called, loud enough that people turned to look at her.

Cliff was staring at her, grinning, as she watched them go huddle by the window. Even from here, Cliff knew they were having a discussion, or maybe interrogation. Beth was clearly not letting him off the hook as Kevin tried to explain with his hands because he couldn't get a word in edgewise.

Cliff leaned back in his chair and folded his arms. Angry didn't even begin to describe how he felt right now. He had thought she had finally saw Kevin for the jerk he was, and now this.

"What the fuck, Luce? You said yesterday you were over him."

"I don't know." Lucy shrugged as if she really had no idea.

"No wonder you were acting off. Another fucking break-up with that loser." Cliff shook his head in disgust. "How many times has it been now, Luce?" he demanded. Too many for him to count.

"Too many." She sighed. "I hope this was the last time."

"Me too. You need to find someone better than him. You are so much better than Kevin; always have been. And don't pull your, *'He got me'* shit. He never got you," Cliff said as he slid his hand up the outside of her shirt and rubbed her neck, hoping that she would listen to him this time.

"I know. I'm just bad at picking guys."

Cliff was stunned at her admission. She had never admitted anything like that before.

In the year since they had met, she had dated loser after loser, each one progressively worse than the last. Then she reconnected with Kevin, who had screwed her over in high school, and she was willing to let him do it again. And again.

"Let me pick the next one. I know how to pick good ones." Cliff continued to caress her back and rub her neck as they talked but didn't feel her relax one bit. Not like she usually did, at least. Then again, usually he didn't enjoy touching her so much.

"What makes you think you can pick a good one? I don't see you in a relationship." Her head flopped forward, letting his fingers work.

"I don't want a relationship, so I stay away from those that do."

Turning her so he could rub her neck with both hands, her muscles finally let go of some of the tension.

"I don't know if I want you finding me a guy," Lucy said, her voice husky.

"Let's see what I find before you immediately shoot the idea down. Might be the best sex of your life, and not just because it'd be vacation sex, which is the best sex ever." Cliff grinned at her, even if she couldn't see.

"How about when we get back? No use looking in Florida." Lucy leaned away from him slowly, as if she didn't want the touching to stop. He knew he didn't.

"You need to get laid by someone who isn't that loser, Luce. I'll find you that guy." He let his hand drop from her back but missed the warm skin under his hand.

"I just need a vacation, Cliff." She looked out the window, or maybe at Kevin the dick and Beth, now back in his arms. Whatever he said had been enough for her to forgive him.

"More than those two?" Cliff leaned back in his chair and took her hand.

"More," she agreed.

"Work or just Mabel again?" he asked, and she stiffened. "Mabel then. She can be a righteous bitch sometimes."

"Sometimes?" she asked, her voice cracking a little.

"Almost always. What did she do now? Did she call you dumb again? Or did she call you lazy even if you work stupidly long hours with Harper and the cleaning job when you don't have a gig?" He squeezed her hand.

Over the last year, he had figured out which of Lucy's sisters were his favorite. In order of most to least, Cliff liked Agatha, the dark horse in the race. Then was Sera, their mom, who was easy to tease and just as easy to get riled up. Next came Buzz, who was always up for a good time. Then it was usually Harper, who was a bitch, but usually a fair one. Last but not least was Lucy's twin, Mabel, who was the most unlovely of them all. If they weren't identical, he would be sure she had been switched at birth.

Not that he knew Mabel well, she never joined in when the rest of the Lovely women went out. And when everyone was waitressing for Harper and Lucy's catering business for Harper and Lucy, she was not there. Even when he had visited Lucy at their home, Mabel was usually missing from the group.

"No, it's not her," she whispered as their flight was called over the loudspeaker.

"That's what you always say, but whenever you get down, it's because Miss Perfect has said something." Cliff got to his feet and grabbed her bag along with his own.

Mabel took every opportunity to remind Lucy that she was more important and smarter. And Lucy listened to her, even if it wasn't true.

"You don't understand." She got up and followed him.

"Being twins doesn't give her the right to talk to you like she does." Cliff turned and walked backward, not caring as he ran into people. "She's just mean sometimes, Luce."

"She doesn't mean to be." Lucy's quiet words were aimed more at the floor than to him, but he heard them.

"Doesn't she? Isn't she the only one who always brings up your failings? Your lack of whatever she thinks you should be?" he said as they made it to the boarding line and stopped and dropped their bags between them.

"Let's talk about something else," she suggested as he looked down at her in confusion. She loved to complain about her sister.

"Okay, then. What about Kevin in your bed? If I hear about that happening again, I'll have to change my rules on hitting women, because you'll need the sense knocked into you." Cliff teasingly tapped his hand to her head. Her dark brown hair was braided today and ran down her back. She rarely wore it that way unless she was catering. She usually preferred a simple ponytail or to just leave it loose.

"Go ahead, I deserve it." She smiled a little and shut her eyes. Instead of hitting her, he poked her nose with his finger, which caused her eyes to open.

"You're too cute and smart to waste any time on that moron. We've discussed this before. Lucy can do better than Kevin. Lucy can do better than Kevin. Lucy shouldn't waste her time on Kevin," Cliff repeated like a mantra. She was still not acting like herself, but at least he got her to smile.

The boarding line was crawling toward the plane, so he kicked their bags the foot forward. It was going to take forever to get on the plane today. Kevin and Beth were a few people behind them in line, being annoying. Since they'd hooked up, they were nothing but touching and kissing all the time, or maybe just all the time they were with Cliff and Lucy. Not that he cared. Beth was just a woman he slept with for a while, but Lucy was still hung up on Kevin. Lucy always fell for guys who liked her—fast. All it took for Lucy to be interested in a guy was for him to notice her. Then, she'd be devastated and clingy when they wanted out.

It had been a long summer of Kevin and Lucy breaking up and getting back together. Kevin was a drummer who wasn't even in a band; he just filled in for bands that needed a drummer. He had no ambition, and Lucy spent all her time trying to get her business going, which allowed the slimeball to cheat on her without her knowledge all the time.

Lucy and Harper spent all their time building their catering business and even managed to work second jobs. Lucy cleaned offices, and Harper worked in an office with weird hours. Both were completely focused on keeping their business going.

Lucy's biggest issue was nobody saw her as smart as she was. Sure, she had a hard time in school, and reading wasn't her thing, but she had booked seventy-five perfect of their catering jobs in the last few months and made a lot of the food. Once Harper showed her how to make a dish, she never forgot and sometimes even improved it.

Lucy's twin was another issue. Mabel taught school and looked down on Lucy, who had struggled to get her GED and never went to college. College wasn't for everyone. Cliff himself had wasted six years in college, and he was a bartender. It didn't matter.

He caught Kevin's eye, and he watched Kevin pull Beth close to kiss her, a little too deeply for a public place as his hand slid into her shorts. Gross, there were kids around.

"Did you want to fake a relationship for those morons?" His chin jutted out to the back of the line as he kicked their bags forward a little more.

Her eyes went wide. She was cute when she acted all innocent. Not that she did it much, but today, she was laying it on thick. With his free hand, he grabbed her by the neck, pulled her to him, and kissed her forehead. His lips lingered a moment too long as he breathed her perfume and hair products that were completely unfamiliar, yet so tantalizing, he wanted to keep smelling her.

"Are they worth it?" Her voice was husky and made Cliff's dick stir like it had never done for Lucy before. Sure, he loved her, but not that way.

"They aren't, but they can't win. We make a way better couple than they do. We were always the cute ones in those relationships." His hand remained on her neck as he took a step backward when the line moved. He couldn't seem to remove it.

The line that should have produced a full laugh only garnered a half-smile. How could a small quirk of her lips be enough to send his thoughts straight to her in his bed? Suddenly, he was back in that dark room lit only by moonlight, sliding his dick into her warm, wet folds as she had that exact half-smile on her lips.

Dropping his hand as if she had burned him, Cliff pushed the thought out of his mind. That had been a drunken mistake, and Lucy didn't even remember it. Nor did he most days; it had been months since it happened and had never been close to repeating it, no matter how drunk they got. Until today. Today he suddenly wanted her.

"I think we just drop it, Cliff. After the plane ride, we won't even see them until we come back," Lucy said. She didn't seem affected by the moment like he was.

"Except their room is right next to ours," he reminded her.

"Ours? We're sharing a room?" she squeaked, as if she didn't know that.

"You were with Kevin when we planned this." It was like she had forgotten all the hours they spent organizing this trip. Sure, she had been drinking most of the time, but she was usually better at remembering things than this.

"I forgot," she said quietly before pointing at him with a motion to turn around.

Handing the ticket to the flight attendant at the doorway, he headed onto the plane with Lucy behind him, which was good because the more time he spent looking at her, the cuter she got—and Lucy wasn't cute. Well yes, she was, but not in *that* way.

He led her all the way to the back of the plane. At the final row, he shoved their bags in the overhead bins as she ducked under him and sat by the window and settled in. Sitting in the middle seat, he asked, "Want me to sit by the window?"

"No, I like the window," she responded without turning to look out of it.

"You hate the window seat. You prefer to not see the ground racing toward us in a crash." He had flown with her twice, and both times she wanted the aisle seat and had never even glanced at the window.

"I'm okay," was all she said as she closed the little shade. Today her usual chatter was silent, and he didn't realize how much he would miss it. Her straight-to-the-point answers were more confusing than her usual meandering off-topic ones because he knew for a fact she wasn't okay.

"No, you are not. I'll get you a drink as soon as we can get one. That will bring Lucy back." Whatever was causing her to be off, alcohol could improve it. The more, the better.

"There might not be enough alcohol on this plane for that," she mumbled as she pulled out her phone and checked for messages.

"I take that as a challenge." He leaned back to watch others boarding the plane. Kevin and Beth were still all hands when they sat in the row in front of them, choosing an aisle seat and a middle one. He could request that they switch seats, but Lucy didn't seem to hate the window seat today.

Feeling squashed in the little seat, he lifted the armrest between himself and Lucy to give him some more room. His leg now pressed firmly to hers, so she scooted away a little but had nowhere to go, so Cliff was pleased when she finally settled in and relaxed.

"Are you going to ignore me the entire flight, dear?" He looked at her staring resolutely at her phone.

"No, sweetie, just while I can still be on my phone." She didn't even look up as she said it.

Grabbing her phone from her, he slid the device into his pocket furthest from her. Knowing she would go digging for it if she wanted to, but since she was acting more subdued, she might not. But he wasn't taking chances. "I will not be ignored."

"Cliff, give me my phone," she demanded as she stared him down.

It was a glimmer of the old Lucy if the Lucy of twenty-four hours ago was the old one. Maybe something happened that he didn't know about before the trip? What if something was happening with one of her sisters that he didn't know about. Or something with her business? He was just going to be supportive until she told him. A friend.

"When we land. You can't play with it on the plane anyway." He put his hand over his pocket in case she went for it. She was, after all, a Lovely.

"I just want it now while we're still on the ground." She held out her hand like he was actually going to put it there. Like he would just return it to her because she asked. That wasn't how this game was played; she knew that.

Leaning forward, he grabbed her thumb and sucked it into his mouth. Instantly all his concentration went to her hand and that thumb. When had Lucy's fingers become so fascinating or so succulent? His tongue caressed and suckled on the thumb as his hands caressed her skin. One hand laced their fingers together while the other trailed down her arm.

A sudden jerk had her pulling her hand away from him. With all his strength, he stopped himself from pulling her onto his lap and kissing her mouth, touching her body, and sliding inside her again. He wanted to see that sexy half-smile again.

As the plane started to move, she sat turned away from him as much as possible as she looked out the window. Arms crossed, she ignored him, which was just fine because he had to get his dick under control. Lucy was supposed to be just Lucy, a buddy to pal around with when he wanted a friend. But today, all he could think about was how sexy she was.

Cliff rationalized that the change was because she was acting differently. If she would just act like Lucy, he wouldn't think of her as a desirable woman. But no, this depressed version of Lucy was turning him on.

After he and Beth and Lucy and Kevin had broken up, he had thought about canceling the trip entirely, but then he had wanted Lucy to get away from work and her sisters for a few days. At the time, he hadn't thought it would be weird if they went alone. The only issue would be avoiding Kevin and Beth for a few days. But after this unexpected reaction to Lucy, Cliff knew he should have just gone alone.

CHAPTER FOUR

WHILE STARING OUT THE WINDOW, Mabel tried her best to ignore Cliff, who seemed to be taking up the entire plane. His leg had taken over her side of the seat, and his arm was hogging the place the armrest should have been. And the way he had sucked on her thumb had made her body long to find out what he could do to more than just her thumb. The entire plane now felt hot and stuffy—no way was she the only one suddenly feeling overheated.

Channeling her inner Lucy was getting harder and harder all the time. Lucy made being carefree look easy. Mabel had never thought that Lucy had a care in the world. She loved cooking and partying, and that was all.

Listening to the drone of the plane engines, she tried to remember if she had been a bitch to Lucy. Was she always putting her twin sister down? Cliff had said if it wasn't her job that Lucy complained about—it was Mabel, which meant Lucy had talked to him about her a lot.

It upset her that she had hurt her sister; she was her best friend. Maybe they didn't always get along, but at the end of the day, they were a pair. Together from the beginning. Mabel and Lucy against the world!

But somehow, over the last few years, they had drifted apart. Even if they only lived across the hall from each other, some days, Mabel didn't see Lucy. Some days Mabel had to admit she didn't *want* to see Lucy. They were opposites in every way, and sometimes Mabel just didn't want her opposite around. But she loved her sister and wanted nothing but the best for her: the best jobs, the best guys, the best everything.

"So how are we going to take on St. Pete Beach?" Cliff asked, his leg bouncing, reminding her that if she was going to be Lucy, she had to act the part. Mabel started tapping her fingers against her thigh in imitation of her sister's constant motion.

"Like the allies going into Normandy," she quipped, then bit her lip. That didn't sound like Lucy at all. To anyone, that was a dead give-away that she wasn't Lucy. Lucy wouldn't watch anything that didn't make her laugh.

"Okay, been saving that one? Is it from a movie?" he asked with a chuckle, not catching her slip-up.

"Yes, something I watched last week," she lied, hoping he wouldn't notice. She really hoped he wouldn't ask which one because Mabel had no clue which movie it could possibly be from.

"I was thinking we'd drop our stuff off at the hotel and then find the closest bar. One we can walk to because we're going to be too drunk to drive." Cliff bumped her shoulder with his.

"I was thinking sleep, then start fresh with booze tomorrow." No need to start with alcohol right away. Or with him at all, if she could help it. Getting drunk had stopped being her thing a long time ago. Not that anyone noticed.

"Nope, no wasting vacation time sleeping. We can go home and do that," Cliff chastised her. "Plus, we have to find you a man. A decent man to make you forget about that ass."

"I want to put that off until later. And since we're sharing a room, what am I supposed to do with this mystery man in our room?" She did not want to have sex on this vacation with a stranger, or anyone for that matter.

"I will sleep on the beach just so you can get laid, Luce. Anything for you." He squeezed her thigh, and she tried not to notice how her mind had that hand slipping higher. "With any luck, you'll have forgotten him by sunrise."

"How's work going?" Mabel changed the subject, hoping to get him to stop talking about her having sex, especially if he was going to touch her while he was talking about it. She was having a hard time not combining the two in her head, and she couldn't forget she was supposed to be Lucy. Or how much Cliff didn't like Mabel.

"Shitty, but I do it almost every day," he said with a grin. "How's old Harps treating you?"

She chuckled at "old Harps." Harper was barely two years older than the twins but had always had the bossiness of a first-born. And for two years, she had treated Lucy like garbage while she worked for her. But after Lucy almost quit, she changed and let Lucy contribute more to their business; cook more and find more events. Lucy was more of a people person, and it showed.

"Good as can be. Harper is Harper," Mabel hedged. She had no idea how work was going for her sister. Lucy always ignored her when she asked or brought it up lately. Maybe it wasn't going well anymore.

"My second least favorite of your sisters. You should show both of them and start your own catering company called Lucy's Luscious Desserts. Because you make the best ones ever," Cliff said, taking Mabel by complete surprise. Would Lucy leave Harper and start her own company?

"And we both know why that wouldn't work out so well." Mabel tried not to be hard on her sister and her problems, but some did stand in her twin's way. She had weaknesses that were obvious.

"No, we both don't. Only you do. I think you can do it. I will help in the beginning." He reached up and cupped the top of her head and lightly massaged it.

"How will you help?" she demanded, pulling away from him, forgetting she maybe should know the answer to that one.

"I can read for you," he stated like it was obvious.

"I can read, Cliff!" she replied. If Lucy couldn't read, she would be the first person to know. Not this nitwit.

"Okay, Luce. You're cured then. Good for you, overcoming your disability after knowing what it is for only a few months. A lifetime of struggle, and how easily you're fixed. And all by yourself." Cliff did a slow clap, and everyone turned around to look at them.

"Don't call it a disability," she hissed. Her sister was not disabled. So, she had had a hard time with school, and they always put her in remedial classes. That wasn't her; she was smart and funny and nothing like those kids.

"Have you read up on it, now that you can read and all?" Cliff stopped making noise.

"No," she admitted since she had no idea what he was talking about.

"I should write a press release about how Lucy Maud Montgomery Lovely has cured herself of dyslexia. She can read now. A miracle," Cliff grumbled, his anger obvious.

"I can read!" she said again, wanting to stand up for her sister, who was not there to defend herself.

"Then this entire weekend, you do not get to order the special. You have order off the menu and read what it says," Cliff stated, holding up one finger.

He was right. Lucy always ordered the special—always had. Sometimes Mabel knew that she didn't like it and ate it anyway. And never had she seen her look through a menu or a cookbook even though she was a chef. Harper was obsessed with them.

Another finger went up. "You must read out loud every text you get. No using that fun read-it-to-me app."

Mabel had never even heard of such a thing; how long had her sister been using it? Why hadn't she ever told Mabel about it?

A third finger went up. "At random, I will ask you to spell something, like a spelling bee."

Mabel couldn't stop herself from running a hand over her Cancan shirt. Lucy's T-shirt printing business had failed because she couldn't spell. The more Mabel thought about it, she realized many of the words were jumbled with letters that looked similar to the right letter.

At that moment, she longed for her phone so that she could read more about what dyslexia was and how to cure it. Because she wanted her sister cured as soon as possible. Words and reading were Mabel's lifeblood, but were they her twin's kryptonite?

"Stop it, Cliff. Leave me alone." Unable to take any more, Mabel yelled and turned away from him.

"Just saying, Luce," Cliff mumbled from behind her.

Mabel watched the ground disappear from under the plane, just like it was crumbling under everything that Mabel knew about her twin sister. Was it possible that Lucy had dyslexia? Was it possible that no one had ever known she had it? Even her?

From school to work, Lucy had struggled in one way or another. Nothing she did came easy.

Like two sides of the same twin coin, the things Lucy had never struggled with were usually what came the hardest for Mabel, like making and keeping friends, letting herself go and being a part of the crowd. Lucy always made her interactions with others look easy and effortless; something Mabel had never been able to replicate.

Cliff reached his arm around Mabel and pulled her close to him. Reluctantly, she rested her head against his shoulder and closed her eyes, letting her mind run through her life with Lucy and all her struggles. Those struggles had made her who she was today.

<h1 style="text-align: center;">CHAPTER FIVE</h1>

CLIFF KNEW Lucy had fallen asleep when her hand fell onto his lap, right onto his penis, which had noticed the slight weight right away. A penis that didn't seem to care that it was Lucy's hand. His Lucy, but he'd never thought of her that way.

Picking up and moving her hand, he tried to put Lucy back in the "just friend's" box. Why she was suddenly not in that box, he didn't know. Hell, he had slept in her bed more times in the last year than he had slept in his own, and never had he even thought of touching her. No matter how drunk he was, she was just there.

From the moment she had landed in his arms at the bar all those months ago, he hadn't thought of her as anything but a buddy. Over the last year, sex with her had never crossed his mind. Even after they had drunkenly had sex that one time, he hadn't wanted to repeat it ... until today.

Since they had met, they had been on numerous little vacations together, at least when she got free from Harper and the demands of catering. They had plans to see the world together. From a two-day whirlwind trip to California to a three-day adventure to see the Grand Canyon in their matching "Grand Cannon" T-shirts. Every time they were together, Lucy was the life of the party, and adventure was her middle name.

She was always the first one to get on the stage for karaoke or climb on the bar to dance. If it was on her mind, it spilled out of her mouth, whether it should have or not. Unpredictable and hardworking were Lucy to a fault.

Not once did he think about hitting on her or sleeping with her; they had been friends for months, and he had learned to enjoy having a woman who was just a friend. It was something he hadn't had much over the years. Most of the time, she was just one of the guys, someone to drink with and go out on the town with, though he did feel more protective of her than his usual friends.

Until today. Today all he could think about was that night, as if it was the only thing that they had ever shared. None of the other times they had been out together even crossed his mind. None of the late nights talking or any of the loud parties or the hours spent at her house watching movies with her sisters. Just her lips on his, then his lips on her body.

It was months ago, and he usually didn't think about it. But ever since he had sat next to her in the airport, it felt like it had happened yesterday. After a late night at work bartending, he was ready to just crash. Lucy had gone home hours before but had said he could crash at the Lovely house when he got off. So, he did, because he loved that house and almost everyone in it.

Quietly, he had gone into the house and up the stairs so as not to wake anyone. Their house was always full of women, and sometimes the men they brought home too. Slipping into Lucy's room, he took off his clothes down to his boxers as she rolled over. He had done it many times and that night was no different.

Until he slid under the covers that were warm from her body. She had rolled his way and snuggled into his body—not a typical Lucy move. Lucy was always moving around when sleeping, and she was a cover thief, not a snuggler. But he let her do it because she was Lucy, and if she needed a snuggle, he would provide it. That's what friends did.

With her body so close, he felt her heat sear into him as he realized she was not wearing a T-shirt like she always did when he stayed over. Her naked breasts were pressed tightly to his chest, tight enough he could feel her pert nipples. Her hand that had been lazily sliding across his stomach was now running up his chest.

Her room was familiar, but the scent of her that night was not. It was something different, something more intoxicating than anything he'd ever experienced.

The combination had him as erect as he had never been in for his friend. She must have sensed what he was feeling and thinking because her hand traveled down his chest and stomach and over his boxers to feel his erection. Suppressing a groan, her head lifted, and she looked him in the eyes.

Her brown eyes were the same as always, except they were dark with desire for him. She had kissed him first, instantly hard and demanding, leaving no question as to what she wanted. His response was to kiss her back because his body and soul wanted her at that moment.

Her hands slid up his chest and pushed him into the mattress, and she rolled over him, straddling him as they continued to kiss, her heat on his erection. Even though his boxers, he could feel how wet she was, how ready she was for him.

Hands cupping her breasts, she rocked slowly over his erection, exquisite friction making him harder. Breaking the kiss, his mouth sought her pert nipples in the moonlight. Lucy had laid one hand on his chest for balance and used the other on his head, lifting him to her breast. His suckling made her groan and grind herself onto his erection even more.

As his mouth moved from one breast to the other, his hands grabbed her thong and pulled it from her body. The material tore easily, and he was able to cup her heat with his bare hand, reveling in her hot wetness. Her moans filled the room as his fingers found her clit, and she rode his hand. She was as responsive as anyone he had been with, more so.

His hand felt the orgasm before her body started to tremor and shake as she moaned his name. Her eyes were half-closed in the moonlight as the tremors slowed and stopped. Pulling his hand away from her, he took his boxers off. In one movement, he slid his penis right into her heat. Eyes on hers as he slid home, watching her half-closed eyes and soft grin as their bodies joined together.

She rode him hard, and he enjoyed the view of her breasts bouncing and her hands in her hair until he couldn't control it anymore and his own orgasm ripped through him. It sent her over the edge again, and he saw stars as she clamped around him, adding to the intensity like nothing he had felt before.

Rolling them onto their sides, they lay there in the aftermath, sated and exhausted. Neither spoke about what just happened, but maybe that was because neither had the breath to speak before they both fell asleep, still wrapped in each other's arms.

When he had woken, she had been gone. It was midmorning, and she was nowhere to be found. Only Sera and the little sisters were in the house. So, he had left and decided to call her, but didn't because he wanted to talk to her about what happened in person. It had been more then sex for Cliff, and he had hoped she felt the same, that she felt the connection also.

But it took Cliff over a day to find Lucy, and when he did, she pretended their night together never happened. And then she looked confused when he sort of brought it up. She had never once brought it up again and he was sure not going to. The sex had blown his mind but hadn't registered in hers at all.

Eventually, his body forgot what she had done to him, most of the time. Not once had his dick even noticed she was near. Or at least until today, when it was thinking about nothing else.

And now he was spending four days with her alone in a hotel room. How was he going to keep his hands off his best friend? He couldn't even keep them off her on the plane ride there.

CHAPTER SIX

It was the dream from her nap mixed with the memories from the night she had sex with Cliff that had her body humming when she woke up. As she woke, she realized she was sleeping on Cliff with his arm around her and her hand cupping his penis. A very large, very hard penis.

Snatching it away and sitting up quickly, Mabel was happy the seat next to Cliff was empty. No one saw her groping Cliff, but no way had he not noticed. Proof had been in her hand that he had.

"Have a good nap?" he asked, less playful than normal, and his voice sent shivers down her spine.

"Yes, thank you," was all Mabel could answer with a small smile, trying to sound normal.

His arm was still slung over her, and his fingers were lazily rubbing her shoulder. It was just enough to keep her body tuned to his. Or maybe it was his scent that had filled their small space in the back of the plane, reminding her of that night long ago.

As if he knew what she was thinking, Cliff leaned toward her. For a kiss? She didn't know until she felt his hot breath on her ear, sending more shivers through her body, this time more southward. "Go with me on this."

Without any idea what he was talking about, she yelped a little as he dragged her body across his until she was straddling the same erection she had just been holding. Except now it was closer to where she wanted to feel it, needed to feel it.

"Kev is watching." He whispered as his arms went around her, touching the bare skin above her jeans. The other traveled up her bare back under her T-shirt. His movements were natural, as if he touched her like this every day. Which she was sure he did not.

Knowing that this would have to look real for Kevin and wanting to touch him with every fiber of her being, her hands slid over his shoulders and then slightly down his back as she leaned closer to him. Their eyes met, and she wondered if she looked as turned on as he did. She certainly felt as turned on as he looked.

Though it had been his idea, she went with it and let go of every thought in her head as her lips brushed his, which was a mistake because the memory of their night together slammed into her, and suddenly one taste wasn't enough. She needed more.

Cliff must have felt the same as his mouth took over, and the kiss turned hot in an instant just like that night. His tongue slid into her mouth, and she moaned at the sweet taste of him. Her tongue met his, demanding for more.

"Excuse me, you must stop," a voice was saying far, far away.

Cliff pulled his mouth from hers, and she hoped he hadn't heard the whimper she couldn't hold back. He looked past her. "Sorry."

At his apology, she turned and saw a flight attendant glaring at them. The woman was tall and blonde and reminded Mabel of her junior high principal, who had hated her. Sliding back into her seat, she knew the kiss had gotten out of hand quickly.

"Sorry," she added, biting her tongue so not add a reflexive "Mrs. Bradley." Lucy had been the troublemaker, but Mabel had been roped in more times than she'd liked to admit by her twin.

"I just asked her to marry me," Cliff said loud enough for Kevin and Beth to hear. With a smile, he pulled her back to him and added, "She said yes."

Mrs. Bradley's twin's scowl turned into a huge smile as she looked between them. It seemed Cliff knew exactly what made stewardesses happy. "Well, congratulations, but none of that on the plane, please."

"If you allow me to kiss her one more time, I'll buy the entire plane a drink," Cliff stated as he lifted himself from the seat without letting Mabel go to pull out his wallet.

What did he say? It was going to cost hundreds of dollars to buy everyone on the plane a drink. Just for one kiss? From her? Did she even want another kiss from him?

The flight attendant smiled at him. "I'll take that offer. You can even kiss her until the drinks are done being served. I don't think anyone will mind, but keep your clothes on or there will be consequences."

Flipping his wallet open with just one hand, Cliff handed her a black credit card. With a spring in her step, the flight attendant went to serve the entire plane drinks. Sadly, not starting with them, because a drink would have made this entire scene make more sense for Mabel.

"You cannot afford to buy everyone drinks," she whispered in case the stewardess heard and came back with Cliff's card.

"You only get engaged once, Luce. Live it up."

Rolling her eyes at him, she said, "You are crazy."

"Crazy for not kissing you last year. Or even last fucking week," Cliff replied, pulling her back onto his lap. Her body didn't even fight him at all, such a traitor.

"There's nothing going on. We're just friends." She tried to get her sister's friendship back on track, hating herself for finding the man attractive and possibly destroying her sister's friendship. No matter what had happened between Lucy and Kirk Langley, Mabel didn't think Lucy deserved to lose her best friend over it.

"Friends who are engaged." He grinned as he cupped her cheeks and rubbed his nose against hers for a moment.

"Not really," she whispered.

Instead of answering, he lightly kissed her lips. Then did it again before they settled, and he deepened the kiss and pulled her closer.

Mabel was powerless to stop the onslaught of feeling since her body wasn't listening to her brain.

His tongue swept across her mouth and continued on as her own body demanded more. A touch or caress, but she didn't want to get in trouble again.

"I think that worked." Cliff nodded at Kevin, who had been watching their heated embrace, or at least until he got caught looking at them.

"Yes, it did," she agreed, realizing he had only kissed her to piss Kevin off. Not because he had wanted to kiss her ... or Lucy since he still thought she was her twin.

He thought Mabel was back home, being judgy and annoying and nobody he wanted to know. Or kiss.

Turning back to the window, she tapped her fingers on her lap, not just because it was what Lucy would do but because she had to think. Somehow, she had to get away from Cliff for the next four days.

No way would Lucy forgive her for having sex with her friend. Since the sisters, all of them, had started dating, there had been a rule of no going after your sisters' boyfriend or exes. So far, it had never been an issue. Mabel always liked the preppy guys, and no one but Buzz liked that type. But Cliff was Lucy's friend, and she didn't know if they had ever dated or had sex. Yes, she had accidentally had sex with him once, but she hadn't meant to do that.

Okay, "accidentally" was a stretch. For months, she had thought that Cliff was sexy, but his personality was a turnoff. The night she had slept in Lucy's bed, and he'd shown up, she had taken advantage of him. Even she knew that. Having him just that once had been worth it, until she hadn't wanted to date for months afterwards.

"Everyone's wondering if there is a ring?" The flight attendant was back, handing them champagne glasses.

"Not yet. I couldn't pick it out without her input. She's a perfectionist," Cliff said, and Mabel wasn't sure if he was talking about her or her sister, though the description was more Mabel than Lucy.

"So sweet," she said and walked away.

Mabel folded her arms. "I will have you know I want big diamonds."

"I know, dear. You need to flash our wealth." He chuckled.

"Now you have the entire plane thinking we're engaged," she whispered, trying to sound angry.

"They're all jealous." He took her hand in his.

"Some are, but some probably think you're an idiot," she pointed out, gesturing to the free drinks everyone was clearly enjoying. All on his dime, the ones he earned as a badly paid bartender.

"Let them," was all he said as he started to play with her hand.

Mabel let him look it over and touch her skin with his other hand as she had seen him do so often with Lucy. Not because his touch felt good, but because he seemed to enjoy it.

"What happened here?" He pointed to a scar on her palm.

"Mabel stabbed me with a pencil when we were ten." In reality, Lucy had done the damage. She had failed the same test Mabel had aced. Lucy had never been able to control her emotions.

Now Mabel viewed the memory in a new light. Lucy had been acting out because she wasn't able to catch on as easily as Mabel had. School was always hard for Lucy, even the easiest of subjects. Was Cliff right that her sister had an actual learning disability?

"She's been mean to you forever," he said, kissing it.

"We've been mean to each other. We fight." It was the truth. All the sisters fought, not just the twins, but the twins seemed to be able to turn on each other instantly. Still, they were willing to back each other to the death at a moment's notice.

"Do you lose track of who you are when you fight? Does her body blend with yours?" he teased.

"We don't look alike," she said reflexively, the same thing they always did when anyone mentioned their similarities. But if they didn't, Mabel wouldn't be on the plane right now.

"You're right. You look more like Buzz." He chuckled.

"Harper," she said quietly. If he had been paying attention, Cliff might've noticed that she had messed up again. Lucy always said Mabel looked most like their redheaded sister, and Mabel always compared herself to the blonde. Though in reality, they bore little resemblance to anyone but each other.

They lapsed into silence as the plane landed in Florida. Looking out the window, she tried to see anything, but it was completely dark. This was the first time she had ever been there. The disappointment at not seeing where they were was only overshadowed by the realization that being on the plane was easy. Being Lucy in Florida was going to be hard.

They remained seated as the plane landed, and the other passengers started to get off. Cliff dug her phone from his pocket and handed it to her as they waited. But she didn't go on it, even though she desperately wanted to. If Lucy really had a disability, she would not look at her phone and never read on it. They were alone before Cliff got up and pulled down their bags. With the bags over his shoulder, he reached over and grabbed her hand, not letting go of her as she followed him off the plane.

In the quiet airport, he led them to the silent car rental offices. She had expected them to take a taxi, but instead, they picked up a tiny little compact car that he barely fit in.

"Where to?" she asked as she got in beside him.

"Hotel and then the nearest bar. You need a drink," he answered, driving the little car away from the airport.

"I don't need a drink," she argued, not wanting to start drinking before she could even relax after the flight.

"Your latest Kevin break-up is even getting me down, Luce. You need tequila." Her sister loved tequila.

"It's after eleven, Cliff. We should just start tomorrow." Not adding that she didn't trust herself to drink and then sleep in the same bed with him, at least not without having sex. She knew her limits.

"You're being a party pooper, Luce. We're only here for a few days, and time is wasting. We need to find you a man. Tonight is the perfect time to start the hunt."

"After getting engaged?" she asked, making him laugh. But she wondered exactly what he was thinking. They had just made out on the plane, and now he wanted her with someone else—a stranger at that.

"I'll use our engagement to fight off the bad ones," Cliff said as he pulled onto the interstate.

"It's just been a long day," Mabel pointed out.

"All days are long when you start out with Kevin in your bed." He didn't look at her when he said it.

"You're right about that," she agreed, glad she had never actually slept with the idiot.

Mabel wished Cliff hadn't reminded her of everything that had transpired that day: Kirk, the phone call, and everything else. All her thoughts were now focused completely on Cliff.

CHAPTER SEVEN

How HAD Cliff managed to find a country music bar in the middle of a beach town like St. Pete? But here they were with matching margaritas at a tall table, watching drunk people dance. The trouble with coming into a bar, sober, at midnight was that everyone else was already drunk.

"See anyone interesting?" he asked, trying not to touch her but finding it impossible after the plane ride.

"Nope," she said, though her eyes had swept the room numerous times since they came in.

"How about the blond surfer dude?" he asked. She was nursing her drink like she was not getting another one when it was gone.

"Which one? Aren't they all blond surfer dudes?" she shot back.

"Good point." He laughed and took a drink as he scanned the crowd again.

The drink was making her cheeks rosy, like when she had been on his lap on the plane. His dick wouldn't easily forget that. Kevin hadn't even been watching, but she had that fucking half-smile when she'd woken up from her nap, and he had to taste it. Nothing would stop him from doing that. And he had paid dearly to do it again, but it had been worth it.

And now they were going to pretend it didn't happen. *Again*. That their kisses weren't the only thing on his mind, and that he wasn't getting pissed with her just looking at other men in the bar. Fuck, she was checking out guys, looking for someone to have sex with, when all he wanted was to have sex with her.

Just as he was about to lean over to tell her that they should leave, one of the tall, blond surfer dudes walked up to them. The surfer only had eyes for Lucy and her chocolate waves. Cliff kicked himself for insisting that she let her hair down when they came into the bar.

"Want to dance?" the surfer asked Lucy, his words a little slurred. Whether he was smashed, or it was due to an accent, Cliff wasn't sure.

"Sure," she said without even looking at Cliff for approval. Not that she hadn't danced with hundreds of others while they were out on the town. This time, though, it was different.

Cliff watched the man take her hand and lead her onto the dance floor as a new slow song started to play. The man's arms wrapped around Lucy, and he grabbed her ass right in front of Cliff. Cliff tried to dull the unfounded jealousy that was coursing through him with a long swallow of alcohol. He had never been jealous of anyone who'd danced with Lucy, and he wasn't about to start feeling that tonight.

When the song finally ended, Lucy stayed in the man's arms as the next song started, saying something with a smile. The man lowered his head toward Lucy's mouth. *Fuck, he was going to kiss her five minutes after they met. In the middle of a bar!*

Off his stool in a flash, Cliff strode over to them and pulled Lucy away from the guy. Both looked at him in confusion. "Lucy, I have to talk to you."

"Lucy?" the man said in confusion.

"Cliff, what do you want?" She willingly let herself get pulled back off the dance floor.

"You don't have the ability to pick the right men, Luce. I'm supposed to be picking guys for you," he reminded her, trying to sound reasonable.

"I didn't pick him; he picked me," she replied flatly.

Cliff led her back to their table. "He was a loser." The blond man, for his part, walked away.

"He was a lawyer," she pointed out.

"What do you have in common with a lawyer?"

"I don't know! You cut in before I could find out." She took a drink of her icy red drink.

"He just wanted to fuck you," Cliff said quietly.

Slamming her glass down, Lucy scowled at him. "Isn't that my goal? To get fucked?"

"Fucked by the right guy; not just any guy," Cliff countered, though any guy would have been okay as long as it wasn't Kevin this morning. Tonight was a different story.

"Are you changing the rules? He really seemed like a good lay."

Cliff could tell she was trying to find him in the crowd.

Cliff saw red. *A good lay?* If all she wanted was a good lay, he was sharing her fucking room. What were they even doing at a bar?

"I'm not changing the rules, but I am trying to keep you safe."

"What about you? Aren't you looking for a good lay?" she demanded.

His eyes stared into her familiar brown ones. He only wanted her right now. No one in this bar even compared to her. Good or bad, he wanted her in his bed.

"This trip isn't about me."

Grabbing her glass, she finished what was left and slammed it on the table. "I'm done. I am tired, and I want to go to bed … alone."

"Fine with me." He pushed his half-drunk glass away. Leave it to a Lovely to outdrink him.

Getting up, she grabbed his drink and finished it off before letting him push her out of the crowded bar. With his hand on her back, he longed to touch her bare skin again.

In the parking lot, he helped her into the rental car. Despite their earlier plan, he hadn't dared let her go to the hotel first. He knew she wouldn't have left the room if they had gone there first, so they had driven straight to the bar. Now he was happy he hadn't had a lot to drink as he drove the few miles to their hotel.

Within minutes they were in the hotel room alone. Now he wished he'd finished his drink when he'd had the chance because the bed dominated the room, and images of her in it dominated his mind.

Once inside, Lucy hurried into the bathroom with only her phone and her carry-on. Somehow, she managed to stay in that room for almost a half an hour, which left Cliff time to organize his stuff and strip down to his boxers, and then spend twenty-five minutes looking at his phone. He couldn't be upset because he needed the time away from her to stop thinking about her and sex at the same time. This was *Lucy*.

When she finally emerged, she looked the exact same, down to the same misspelled T-shirt and jeans she had flown down in. Not that she didn't look adorable in them, just twenty-five minutes in the bathroom was a long time. What she had done in that room was a complete mystery to Cliff.

What he did know was that the alcohol hadn't helped her bad mood. She was still not the Lucy he was accustomed to, the Lucy he knew and loved. And if alcohol wasn't going to get her out of her depression, he had no idea what would.

When it was his turn, Cliff wasted as much time in the bathroom as possible, brushing his teeth slowly and spending way too much time looking at the stuff Lucy had left on the counter. All of it seemed just a little off. Her hairbrush was purple, and he remembered it being blue. Her face soap was a completely different brand, even though she had once lectured him when he had bought her the wrong one. Even her birth control was different than he remembered from other trips. The little plastic case wasn't the same old one as usual.

Picking the medicine up, he looked at it closely and wondered if she had changed, and that was affecting her hormones and thus her mood. It would explain some of what was happening. Probably most of it. *That had to be it*, he decided and tossed it back into her bag and headed out of the bathroom. Problem solved.

Back out in the bedroom, he saw she was under the covers and probably sleeping. Her body wasn't moving. If Lucy was awake, she was moving.

Sliding into bed beside her, the unexpected new smell enveloped him again, not like the same old Lucy at all. He rolled onto his side and looked at the back of her head—she was sleeping on the wrong side of the bed. Could hormones cause that?

It took everything inside him not to pull her into his body and hold her to him, but Lucy wasn't a cuddler and would complain if he woke her up.

Cliff sighed. He had thought that this weekend would just be a fun getaway for both of them after the last busy few months, but this new, added sexual tension was unexpected and making the trip odd. He hoped that after a good night's sleep, everything would right itself between him and Lucy. He couldn't hold out for three more days.

CHAPTER EIGHT

How Cliff had managed to fall asleep with a hard-on, he didn't know, but it woke him early the next morning. Sadly, Lucy was the first thing on his mind when he opened his eyes. On his mind and in his arms.

She was pressed tight to his body, and her T-shirt had ridden high over her hips. Her bare back was pressed to his stomach and chest, and his hand was cupping her breast—with no clothing separating them.

Over the last year, he had slept with this woman so many times he couldn't count, but he had never ever woken up like this. His entire body felt ready to go if she gave just the barest hint that that was what she wanted. A breathy yes, a nod, a twitch.

But she didn't move, so with regret, he slowly let go of her right breast in all its glory and then rolled onto his back, hoping he didn't wake her as he did it. Or hoping he did, so he could feel that breast again, and maybe its twin. Cliff got of bed. He needed to get away from Lucy Lovely and his newfound attraction to her.

Digging in his bag, he pulled on a pair of running shorts and socks, then grabbed his headphones and headed to the door. He knew he needed to run as far and as fast as he could away from her. Not that he wouldn't come back, but he needed a good long run to lecture himself before anything happened. She was Lucy, the same Lucy from back home. Nothing had changed. Except it had somehow.

Music up loud, he ran until he couldn't smell her on his skin anymore for the sweat rolling off of him. Then he ran a few more miles. His internal lecture wasn't working; he could still feel her breast in his hand, and he still liked it ... a lot. And memories of that half-smile were ever-present now.

Groaning, he slowed to a walk in a little area of shops. Cliff looked around for something to bring back for breakfast for them since there was no free breakfast, and their dive of a hotel didn't have a restaurant close to it. His eyes landed on a donut shop, and he grinned. Lucy loved sweets. But sometimes she didn't like them so early in the morning. She often preferred to eat leftovers from her catering business for breakfast, but then again, he had seen her eat both at the same time.

Deciding he had better ask if she wanted donuts, he pulled out his phone to call her. If he texted her, she might not hear the notification or just ignore it. He knew a lot about his friend and her likes and dislikes. Looking in the window, he listened to the ringing on the other end, hoping she would at least answer the phone.

"What?" Lucy's sleepy voice was husky as she answered.

After over twelve hours of constant erections from that voice, Cliff suddenly didn't find it quite as sexy or care that she was nearly naked in that bed.

Maybe his lecture had worked, and he was over that weird lust for her. That would be great.

"Hey, Luce. I'm out getting donuts," he said. Finding some leftover pork chops would be impossible, so best not even suggest other options.

"Get me something with lemon in it. And bring it over." He could hear her rolling over in bed but wasn't able to picture it as clearly as before.

Cliff pulled the phone away and looked at it. Over? They were sharing a room. What part of that was over?

"I am in Florida, Luce," he reminded her. Maybe she wasn't that awake yet.

"Fuck! That was this week? I completely spaced it. I am so sorry, Cliff. I'll pay you back for the tickets, I swear." His best friend was going crazy. She was in a hotel staying with him and pretending to be back in Minnesota. That was just like the old Lucy. Everything was a joke to her.

"It's okay. Next time." He went with it. Let her have her fun; they would share a big laugh when he got back to the hotel.

"Are you sure you're not mad? I had this big blow-up with Maby, and she threw all my stuff on the lawn, so I had to spend all day yesterday bringing it back inside. Agatha helped her and wouldn't help me clean up at all, and Harper and Buzz just laughed and went to the Grog," Lucy complained, her story getting more elaborate as she went along.

"And Sera and the little girls?" he asked, referring to her stepmom who, though engaged, still spent a lot of time in the house she shared with her daughters. So far, she and her youngest girls hadn't moved out to live with her fiancé. But she kept saying, "soon."

"They were out with Harrison. It seems supper at Grandma's doesn't include us," Lucy said, but it didn't sound like she was pouting.

"I'm not mad. Just tell Maby to fuck off," he answered, as always. Mabel Lovely was a pain in Lucy's side.

"She might be in the right this time. I really wasn't thinking. But she's hiding from me anyway," Lucy said.

Oddly, that didn't sound like a Lovely reaction: hiding. They were a face-your-challenges type of people. Avoiding a fight with her sister was out of character.

"Well, see you when I get back then." He chuckled. *At the hotel*.

"Please don't me mad. I'll take you out for drinks when you get back, all night. I'll even pay," she promised. They always split the tab when out drinking since they were just buddies.

"Okay, bye, Luce." He shook his head at her.

"Bye, Cliff. Have fun down there." She hung up.

Going into the donut shop, he picked out a lemon one and a chocolate one for himself. Heading back to the hotel at a slower pace, he thought about his conversation with Lucy. She seemed completely different on the phone than all day yesterday. The old Lucy was back. The cadence and the tone of her voice had been the same, but the word choices and emotion behind them were different. Lucy didn't have to be drunk to be Lucy; she was always Lucy. Until yesterday.

Pulling out his phone as he walked, he pulled up the app that could pinpoint the location of Lucy's phone. Right before his eyes, the GPS locator showed him the middle of the Lovely house thousands of miles away from where she actually was. He had even had her phone in his pocket on the plane.

Stopping in the middle of the sidewalk, he realized who was in their hotel room: Mabel Lovely. It had to be Lucy's double, though he hadn't thought they were close enough alike that Mabel could trick him into thinking she was Lucy—*for hours*.

Yes, he knew they were identical twins, but Mabel had always had an attitude about her that Lucy never had. Or had it been an attitude? Because he had enjoyed his time with her yesterday.

Now he was really seeing why he was suddenly attracted to his buddy. She was actually her sister! Her sexy as hell sister, who turned him on in a way his buddy never did.

Cliff set his pace back at a run; he wanted to get back to the hotel before she woke up. There was no way she was getting away with pretending to be Lucy. Not for another minute.

CHAPTER NINE

MABEL WAS READING up on dyslexia as fast as she could. Because after what she had read on it in the bathroom the night before, she knew she couldn't be on her phone in front of Cliff and have him still think she was Lucy. Apparently, everything she was reading Cliff already knew.

When they had gotten back to the hotel last night, she had stolen away and read as much as she could on what Cliff had diagnosed her sister as having. It had taken one article and one small video for Mabel to see he was right; many of the symptoms Lucy had always struggled with. So many quirks about her sister had been explained in twenty minutes, quirks that had puzzled Mabel her entire life.

No matter what, Lucy was never as ditzy as people thought she was. Her personality with her friends and lovers was always flighty and clueless, but with her sisters, she was fun and creative and had ideas that turned out to be golden. Yes, some failed, but she still was willing to try them.

Over the last year, she had been putting more and more effort into what had started as Harper's catering business. It had started growing rapidly because Lucy was seeking out events rather than letting clients come to them. Her twin knew every recipe that the two made for every event by heart and could tell you what they had served months before. Harper counted on Lucy to know the menu for every event they had on schedule, something Harper didn't even know.

But why was it never caught in school? Why were the teachers so quick to let Lucy fail without ever looking into why? Her sister had dropped out of school in the tenth grade because she was going to have to repeat it. From there, she had started working in restaurants as a waitress and moved her way into being a cook. Mostly she had been taught by other cooks while on the job, and more recently, by Harper. But never by reading or taking classes. And Lucy never opened a cookbook.

When they had been twenty, Sera had talked Lucy into trying for her GED, but just before the exam, Mabel had found her crying, saying she would never pass the test. So, Mabel gave her a pep talk and took the test for her twin. Yes, it was wrong, but in the end, it was just a box on a job application—a box that would make a lot of difference in her life, even if she never went to college. Mabel never regretted taking the test for Lucy, and they never told anyone they had switched for it. It was the last time they had switched, until now.

Waking up this morning in an empty bed should have been normal and familiar, but it was cold. The night before, after coming out of the bathroom and Cliff going in, she had changed quickly and climbed into bed and worried about sleeping with Cliff. She had been worried that the alcohol would've been enough to let down her inhibitions, and she would take what she wanted. Because she wanted him badly.

The day had been long, and she had fallen asleep instantly before he even got out of the bathroom. But that didn't mean she wasn't thinking about him; her dreams had been full of him and what he could do to her. Some were rather over the top. Still, waking up alone had been a blessing so Mabel could have time to cool herself down before facing Cliff again. Over the top or not, she wanted to give a few a try with Cliff.

She quickly showered and slid on a pair of jean shorts and a red tank top, half wondering if he had left her for the day. He was coming back since his bag was still on the floor in the corner.

With him gone, she sat down to read more about her sister. She was so deep in reading that she almost forgot to shut it off when the door of the hotel room finally opened.

Setting the device down, she looked up at Cliff coming in the door, which was a mistake because he was shirtless in shorts and had sweat running down his body. Nobody who was a bartender by night and lazy bum by day should look that good without a shirt on.

"I got donuts." He held up a bag, which she couldn't see because her eyes wouldn't leave his glistening body.

"Thanks," she managed to say, but maybe she was thanking him for just being there to look at.

Cliff walked over to the bed and dropped the sack on her stomach. Grabbing it up, she dragged her eyes from him and looked inside. "Which one is yours?"

"The one that isn't your favorite," he responded, looking down at her as if he was testing her.

"Okay, then." She reached into the bag for the donut she did not want, knowing it was full of fake lemon. God, how she wanted the chocolate one. Pretending to be her sister was getting harder. "Are you going to eat before you shower?"

"I don't need a shower, do I? It's vacation; there's no showering on vacation," he responded, shaking his head, making sweat droplets fly through the air and hit her.

"Gross, Cliff." Still holding the bag, she rolled away from him to the other side of the bed—the side that still smelled like him.

"Are you afraid of a little sweat, Lovely?" He climbed onto the bed and chased her.

His advance shocked her, or maybe it was the way his body moved that had her frozen. He climbed on top of her, holding her down with his sweaty body. Grabbing her wrists, he shook the bag from her hands, letting it fall to her side before stretching her arms over her head. She was using all her strength to get out from under him. After years of fighting with her sisters, she should have accomplished it, but he held on to her.

"I think you're losing this battle, Lovely. Prepare to be sweaty," he said but didn't move from his position. His eyes were glued to her breasts and the way they were heaving as she breathed.

She stopped fighting him, well aware that her body was screaming for him to stop looking and start touching. If he dropped her hands, she would do nothing but touch him, all of him.

Under her shoulder, her phone started to ring, bringing her back from the brink. Cliff let go of one of her wrists to grab the phone. Lifting her shoulder, she watched him read the name on the screen.

"Your mom." He dropped her other wrist and handed her the phone. Whatever was about to happen between them was not going to anymore.

Before the next ring, he was off of her and striding toward the bathroom. After watching him slam the door behind him, she hit the button to answer her phone. Mabel felt barely able to move. She could still feel him on her body, pressing her into the bed, all hot and wet and sexy.

"Hi, Sera." She sat up finally, though a little shakier than she'd like to admit.

"Where are you, Maby? Buzz said you didn't come home last night. That's not like you," Sera said. It was true. Her other sisters stayed out all night all the time, but Mabel and Agatha were the homebodies. Agatha often worked nights and was often gone, but Mabel was always home at night.

"Just at a friend's. I needed to get away from Lucy for a while." Keeping her voice down, she eyed the door to the bathroom, where Lucy's friend, not hers, remained.

"I talked to Lucy, and she said nothing happened. I believe her." Sera had tried to settle the twin's fight, like she always did. Sometimes her meddling worked, sometimes not, but she always tried.

"I just need a few days, Sera. I will be home by the weekend. Buzz cannot have my room." Mabel looked out the window to the parking lot. Their room had quite the view.

"She's sleeping in your bed until you get back." The Lovely house was one bedroom short, so Buzz slept on the couch unless someone was out, then she slept in the free bed. Soon she would be getting her own room because Sera was planning to move in with her fiancé. Sera would also take the little girls with her, leaving not one but three bedrooms empty. The house would feel empty then, Mabel was sure.

"Okay. I just need time," she said again.

"Be back by Saturday. I want to go dress shopping."

"You're not still thinking about marrying him, are you?" she teased the woman who had never been serious about a man until Harrison had shown up. Now there was no denying that Sera was all in with the guy. Happily, he was just as smitten with her.

"I should have eloped weeks ago." Sera laughed, but Mabel knew she wasn't completely joking.

"If you weren't so set on a big wedding, Harrison would have married you last month." It was strange to remember that the couple had only been dating a month.

"I waited years for that man, so he can wait a month or so to marry me. I'm already in his bed." Sera chuckled, not caring that she was oversharing.

"Too much information, Mom." Mabel laughed.

"When you want them, Maby, I can give you details that will make your toes curl and question if the sex you had before was actually sex." Sera laughed. This was the mom that had raised her.

"See you in a few days."

"Okay, come back anytime. Lucy will apologize."

"Bye, Sera."

"Bye, Mabel Lucie," her mom said, reminding Mabel of the name she shared with her twin. It was something Sera said every time the twins fought. A little way to remind her that they were once one.

Turning from the window, Mabel sat on the edge of the bed. It was getting harder and harder to pretend to be Lucy with Cliff. After their short wrestling match, Mabel knew that it had turned Cliff on, but was he turned on because she was Lucy? Was he in love with Lucy? Lucy had always denied that they were anything but friends, but did Cliff feel the same way? Was she getting between two people who were falling in love by being here? Was she messing everything up for her sister?

She was still sitting there when Cliff walked out of the bathroom with a towel around his waist. Even now, her fingers itched to pull it away, and she hated herself for it.

"I don't know our plans, but I'm going to go to the beach today," she said, trying to pull her mind away from the towel and everything underneath it.

"No can do, sweetheart. I already have plans for us." He dug in his suitcase and didn't even look her way.

"I just want to see some sun out there." She waved in the general direction of the beach. This was, after all, her vacation. She wanted to relax a little.

"I guarantee you'll see the beach sometime today." He pulled out his swim shorts and held them in the air as if they'd been hiding from him.

"Please, Cliff," she begged. She couldn't spend the day with him.

She turned to him in time to catch the towel fall to the ground, leaving him naked as he pulled his swim trunks on. Being naked in front of her didn't seem to bother him, making her realize Lucy had seen him naked. Probably a ton of times. Which meant *she* should not be seeing him naked, and definitely not enjoying it.

"Nope, you're coming with me today. Do you have your suit on?" He tossed the towel in the general direction of the bathroom, hitting the wall.

Getting up, she grabbed the towel and hung it up in the bathroom to dry. "Yes, I do." She had planned to spend her day at the beach, just not with him. Except now she had to change her plans.

"Are you ready to go then?" Grabbing the donut bag and car keys, he walked out the door, leaving her to follow. No day without Cliff for Mabel.

CHAPTER TEN

HIS ANGER at Lucy's twin had lasted only a few minutes. That was when he realized he had a chance to help out his best friend. He could barely contain his excitement about it. Today he was going to teach Mabel Lovely exactly how her sister lived—AKA, teaching Mabel Lucie Lovely to loosen up.

Over the last year, he had seen Maby, as her sisters called her, only a dozen times. He'd blamed it on the long hours she'd spent working on her masters, then getting a job. He always thought it was likely her education had made her feel superior to the others. Even last month, when the bar he worked at was swamped because of an article that featured it in the paper, all the Lovely girls had worked extra shifts and filled in holes when needed, all except Mabel. Never once did he even think to ask her.

Cliff glanced over as she looked out the car window. Her chocolate hair was up in a ponytail, so much like how Lucy wore hers. But now that he knew it was Mabel, he couldn't see her as Lucy anymore. And what he wanted to do with Mabel was nothing like what he wanted to do with Lucy.

Pulling into a nearly empty parking lot, he wondered if he could get her to admit she was Mabel but decided this was the perfect spot to see her crack: a nude beach. Lucy would die if he took her there, at least unless she had a few drinks in her. Both sisters were very conservative, but he knew Mabel was going to be more so, very much more so.

Both climbed out of the car, and Cliff grabbed the towels from the back seat. Mabel walked ahead of him to get a good spot on the beach, which wasn't going to be an issue since it was nearly empty. With only a few people here and there, there was plenty of room on the beach for them to have privacy. Not that it would take much time for her to want to leave; she wouldn't last a minute before she stormed off if she had to get naked in public.

Catching up with her as she looked around, he chuckled when her eyes landed on an elderly couple sitting a few yards away. They were completely naked. Not the sight that Cliff wanted to see, but worth it to crack Mabel.

"A *nude beach*?" she whispered. Her eyes were now firmly on the water in front of them.

"You wanted a beach, and this was the closest," he lied.

"We drove for almost an hour, Cliff." She called him on his bluff.

Laying out the towels on the sand, he couldn't stop grinning at her discomfort. Pulling off his shirt, he tossed it on one of the towels. "Clothes off, Lovely."

Now that he knew she wasn't Lucy, he couldn't bring himself to call her that. With nothing left, he had decided to use her last name, though it rolled off his tongue too easily for his liking.

"No way," she hissed.

"Scared, Lovely?"

"Of course not," she argued and pulled off her tank top. The purple fabric lifted to reveal an equally purple bikini top. Tossing the shirt on top of his, she shimmied out of her jean shorts.

Over the last year, he had seen Lucy close to naked a few times, but she had never looked this good. Her stomach wasn't this flat with a hint of muscles under it, and her legs didn't go on forever. Nor did her breasts beg him to touch them.

Instead of touching them, he did the next best thing. Reaching behind her, he easily snapped the clasp that held the material covering them together. Before his eyes, the wisp of purple fell to the sand, leaving her glorious pale globes exposed to the hot sun.

His eyes were taking her in, and he expected her to cover them at any moment, but that didn't happen. To his amazement, she turned, shimmied out of her bottoms, and headed to the water—naked as the day she was born.

Cliff desperately wanted to follow, but there was no way he could take off his swim trunks now. His erection was straining to get free and play in the water with her. This had completely backfired on him.

She was a Lovely, and he had yet to find one that wasn't comfortable with their body. So far, after a year, he had seen well over half of them topless. Most of the time in public. They changed shirts with each other at any given moment, and most would flash you. Harper was actually the most prolific flasher of the group; he had seen those babies more than most of her boyfriends had. The first time had been to get a free drink, and then she had forgotten to wear a bra during a few shirt exchanges. But for some reason, he thought that Mabel was different.

Watching naked Mabel frolic in the sand for almost half an hour, he realized she wasn't coming back. So far, she had just stood and let the waves splash against her. Then she swam for a little while, and now she was looking for shells along the beach at the water's edge.

He had been watching her the entire time. Getting up from the towel, he finally went out to her. "You need sunscreen."

"I'm okay," she replied, turning to him, not caring she was naked.

"You're going to get a sunburn." He didn't add, *all over your glorious body*.

"I don't really burn. I just tan nicely." She shrugged and picked up another shell. After looking at it for a moment, she tossed it back into the water.

"The sun is hot here."

"Are you afraid to burn your dick, Cliff? Because your shorts are still on," she pointed out.

"Yes, I am. He's very special to me." He ran his hand over the front of his shorts. Even his own hand on his dick made it quiver with her standing naked in front of him.

"Too bad, the water's nice." She turned to the ocean again. Running his eyes over her back he stopped at her ass, well, just above her ass. The woman had a fucking *tattoo* of her name on her hip. Mabel Lucie Attwell was written right there. He wanted to touch it, but if he did, she would remember the tattoo. Then she would know that he knew, and he wasn't ready for that yet. He had just started his lesson, after all.

As his eyes dipped lower, he wondered how long she's had the tattoo. Long enough that she had to have forgotten it was there when she stripped naked.

"I can still go in, even if I'm not naked," he pointed out.

"Nope, rules are that it's a *naked* beach, Cliff." She took her shells and brushed past him, heading back to their towel. Once there, she dried herself off and then put her clothes back on. "Are you going to feed me?"

"Yeah, sure," he mumbled, unable to stop staring at this woman. Lucy would never have stripped naked in public sober. Drunk, yes, but not sober. But her straightlaced twin had, without a care of who saw. He was starting to think he didn't know the first thing about Mabel.

"Good, because I'm starving." She headed to the car.

Following her like a puppy with his own completely dry towel, Cliff watched her ass swaying in her short shorts. He was afraid he was going to crack long before she did.

In the car, he was trapped with her smell mixed with the scent of the ocean. His mind was on her body and what he wanted to taste first. Whatever it would be, he was sure it would taste salty right now.

Pulling up to a semi-offbeat-looking restaurant, Cliff took Mabel's hand as they walked into the place. It was a dive, but most of the time, the food was good. This wasn't his first time here. When Lucy was the one coming on the trip, he wanted to show her this place because she loved food. With Mabel, he wasn't so sure she'd like it. Maybe he should have taken her to a fancier place.

They were seated outside, per Mabel's request, and had each

ordered a drink: a mixed drink for him, and an iced tea for her. He had thought she would be uncomfortable with the quirky vibe, but she seemed at home. Leaning back in her chair, she watched the traffic drive by.

The waitress came with menus, and Cliff told her, "No need for menus. A burger for me, and the lady will have the special."

They both knew that Lucy's go-to was the special. Even when she didn't know what the special was, she ordered it. Sadly, sometimes she didn't like it at all, but would still eat as much as she could and pretend to like it. All so she wouldn't have to look at a menu and try to read what they offered.

Mabel didn't say anything about the order, just looked out at the street beyond the plastic fencing of the patio area. "Why do you think I have dyslexia?"

Her words surprised him after her vehement denial yesterday. Not bringing up their past discussion on it, because that had been with Lucy, he said, "My uncle had it. He actually got a lot of help for it in school, but he explained it to me once. I was worried it was something else since he was different in other ways too. But anyway, I read up and went to see an expert about it."

"When was this?" She took a drink of her tea.

"Years ago, actually. He committed suicide when I was in high school, over other things. It made me seek answers to the questions that I hadn't cared about before," he admitted. He hadn't ever even told Lucy about Cal, but for some reason, he wanted Mabel to understand that part of him.

"I'm sorry, Cliff. Where you close?"

"Yeah. He lived with my mom and me while I was in high school and college. Since he was only five years older than me, we got close."

"That must've been hard. I don't have any aunts or uncles, but if I lost one of my sisters, I would be devastated."

"It took years to get over. In fact, I still have issues with it today. But when I met you"—he almost stumbled. She was Mabel now, not Lucy—"I saw some of the same issues. Ignoring things that had to be read, not writing things down, or being able to tell me how to make a drink, but not ever finding the correct bottle behind the bar."

"Why do you think the diagnosis was missed?" She leaned on her elbows on the table. Mabel was more interested in the discussion than Lucy had ever been. Her love for her twin was evident, making him think that she wasn't as different from her sister as he had thought. No matter what Cliff said about Mabel, Lucy had defended her every time.

"Because you were a girl, and it affects more boys. Also, the public school system doesn't have time to analyze every student that acts out, which you always did. It was easier to say you were just stupid and put you in remedial classes than find the true reason," he said. He knew the words were true, but he could never be sure why they had missed it when she was in school.

"How old was your uncle when they figured it out?"

"Around eight. By the time he graduated, he could read, but not well."

"What does that mean for me?" Her eyes filled with tears. She clearly knew the answer; she just had to hear him say it.

"You will probably never know how to read any better than you do right now. Unless you work at it," he answered, hating himself for making her cry.

"I want to help," Mabel said, not realizing she had dropped the pretense of being Lucy.

"I have been showing you all kinds of life hacks to get by. But you have to tell your family. They'll never understand if you don't. You need their support," he said.

Before she could reply, their order appeared before them, stopping the conversation in its tracks. Mabel wiped away the tears from her face and looked at the fish meal. Lucy hated fish, but Cliff had no idea what Mabel thought of it. Either she was still pretending to be Lucy and did not eat it, or she didn't like it, because she didn't eat the fish. Everything else, she happily ate.

CHAPTER ELEVEN

Relaxing in a beach chair, Mabel watched the waves crash into the beach. This time yesterday, she was scheming her way to get on a plane for a stolen vacation. Today, she didn't have a care in the world. Okay there were a few cares, but most could be put on the back burner for a day or two.

Cliff was walking along the edge of the water now like he had been doing for close to an hour as she nursed her whiskey Coke that was mostly water now. With a lazy hand, she dumped it into the sand. There would be plenty more drinks today.

Her plan to go off alone had been foiled at every move, mostly because Cliff would not return her to the hotel they were staying at. Mabel was surprised to discover that she was actually having fun with the crazy man. She was starting to see why Lucy liked him so much.

After lunch, he had taken her parasailing, and she'd had a blast, though she had been skeptical at first. One, because she was a little afraid of heights, and two, her swimming skills were lacking to be flying above the ocean. But in the end, Cliff had made her feel safe, and she got to experience something she never would've had she not stowed away on her sister's vacation.

Cliff must have felt her watching him because he waved at her, causing her to wave back. That man was growing on her. Since the first time she'd met had him, Mabel felt like he was annoying and at times smarmy. Most people viewed it as flattering, but not Mabel. Until this vacation.

Her thoughts were broken when a shadow fell across her bare stomach. She had lost her tank top after parasailing and was loving the sun on her skin. Looking up, she rolled her eyes at the loser staring at her breasts, as if his girlfriend wasn't close by.

"Lose your fiancé, Lucy?" Kevin's eyes didn't leave her chest.

"Nope, he's finding me a shell." She waved her hand at the ocean.

"You know, Beth and I have an open relationship." His voice was low. What an ass.

"I knew you would miss this once you no longer had it. But now it is too late. I'm with Cliff." She wasn't pushing the engaged thing because that would never be real.

"Cliff has nothing on me." Kevin winked suggestively.

"You mean his penis? No, his is larger, girthier." She used her hands to demonstrate. "And, of course, he has better moves than you. Orgasms actually happen every time, not just sporadically. And since you don't know what that means, it means almost never."

Kevin's grin faded. "Bull."

Waving her arm at Cliff again, she yelled, "Honey, Kevin wants to see your dick! He's very interested in seeing it!"

"Fuck, lady, stop it." He backed away from her. She knew others at the bar were looking at them now; she didn't even have to turn around. Her twin wasn't the only one blessed with a voice that carried.

"What?" came a yell from the water's edge.

Grinning, she yelled again even louder, "Kevin here wants to see your dick!"

"You're a shit, Lucy." Kevin stormed away from her, leaving her in her happy place: winning a battle of words. Even against a nitwit.

A shirtless Cliff walked toward her with something in his hands. At this point in the day, she should've been pissed at him. So far, he hadn't let her order anything because Lucy let him order all the time.

And he hadn't actually taken her places Lucy would have liked. Lucy hated heights, and Lucy would not go to a nude beach, ever. For a girl who slept around pretty regularly, she was actually pretty conservative about her body. Mabel, on the other hand, had no qualms about getting naked for no reason.

When she had stripped down, she had hoped he would also, but she knew why he didn't. He had a boner the entire time. A boner for Lucy, not Mabel, though, because they had now crossed the twenty-four-hour mark without him knowing it was her.

"Was that Kevin?" he asked when he got close enough.

"Yes, the ass. I told him you have a bigger dick. I hope you don't mind," she stated and enjoyed the lazy grin that spread across his face.

"I hope you said *much* bigger."

"Nope, just slightly."

"But it is much bigger. It's huge."

"Next time we run into them, you guys will just have to pull them out. Compare and contrast." She shrugged.

"I think so too." He sat on the edge of her chair, his butt touching her hip. She scooted over to give him some room, which only caused him to take up more of the chair.

"Have fun in the water?" She closed her eyes. He was so close, she couldn't concentrate on anything except the feel of him pressed against her leg.

"Yep. I found you something." He touched her leg, wordlessly asking her to open her eyes.

Opening them, she looked at his blue eyes and smiled a little at the happiness she found there. Happiness at bringing her a present. Well, bringing *Lucy* a present.

"What?" she managed to question.

"A sand dollar. Have you ever seen one before?" he asked, holding up the round white disk.

"No," she whispered and took it gently from his hand. "Did you find this?"

"Yes, and I thought of you. Were you looking for one this morning?"

In reality, she was looking for a large shell but hadn't found anything really good. But she had seen hundreds of broken shells as she looked.

"I don't know what I was looking for," she admitted.

"Well, you can have this one. Are you done with your drink?" He nodded at the glass.

"Yes, but I'm okay with being done for a while." Though her family was big on social drinking, it hadn't been her thing for years. In fact, she avoided it more when she went out.

"Are you done here? Or just done drinking?" His hand was still on her leg.

"I'm relaxed here."

"You're not going to fall asleep, are you?"

"No." But she was, just for a little while.

"I think you are."

"You've filled my day, Cliff. I'm worn out."

"Let's go dancing! There's a place not far from the hotel. We can walk." Grabbing her hand, he pulled her out of her comfy chair. She reluctantly agreed.

"Oh, Cliff, I'm exhausted." She didn't fight him as he kept going, his hand holding hers.

"Good tunes and a few drinks, and you'll be perfect." He pulled her to the rental car.

Mabel had known it was going to be hard being Lucy, but it was exhausting playing her sister for a day. At least there had been no cooking involved, a talent Mabel couldn't fake.

Less than an hour later, she had another whiskey Coke in her hand. The bar was wall to wall people, but Cliff managed to find an empty table. After setting down her drink, she was immediately asked to dance by a guy at the next table over. With a shrug, she followed him onto the dance floor. After all, this was why they were here.

Halfway through the song, she caught the look on Cliff's face that said he was pissed she was dancing with a guy. Since Mabel wasn't interested in the guy at all with Cliff in the room, she went back to the table once the song ended. The guy didn't seem all that interested either as she sat down next to Cliff, who threw his arm around her and pulled her close. She took a sip of her drink and set it back down, the strong liquid burning as it went down.

"Dance?" he leaned over and said into her ear.

"Sure." Pulling out of his grasp, she walked to the dance floor, creating space between them for the fast song.

Despite the song's tempo, he pulled her tight to him and rocked with her slowly, not following the beat of the music at all. Sighing, she rested her head on his shoulder and went with it because that was exactly where she wanted to be. Wrapped in his arms.

After three more fast songs, they were jostled off the floor by an energetic group of dancers. Shrugging, he took her hand and led her back to the bar and ordered more drinks. Their table was long gone as they stood surrounded by a million people, and not one did she care to talk to besides Cliff.

Taking one drink, she shook her head again at the alcohol content. It burned. Setting the drink on the bar, she leaned into him and yelled, "I'm done."

"Come on, Lovely. You aren't even buzzed yet!" he yelled back.

"I don't want to get buzzed," she confessed.

Yes, she knew that acting like Lucy meant she needed to drink more, but Mabel didn't want to. It had been a long day, and she was tired—too tired to pretend to be her sister anymore.

Slamming his drink down, he hissed over the music, "You aren't even going to drink? That's what this entire vacation is about."

"I'm just not feeling it today, Cliff. It's been a long day." She closed her eyes for a moment, hoping he would pick up on how tired she was.

"Bullshit," he yelled at her. "You almost made it through the entire day, pretending to be Lucy. Almost. But it's harder than you think being her, isn't it?"

"What did you say?" she gasped in shock.

He knew. How long had he known? When did he figure it out? Had he always known? Maybe she wasn't as good at being Lucy as she had thought she was.

CHAPTER TWELVE

MABEL'S shocked expression almost made him laugh. If he wasn't so pissed, it would have. He wasn't even pissed at her; he was pissed at himself and his reaction to her.

"Perfect Mabel can't let go of her control and get drunk, even when she's pretending to be her sister. The one she likes to call a drunk!" Cliff glared at her as a blush rushed up her face.

Of course, it wasn't her fault he was mad. He was pissed at his body for wanting her so much. Watching her dance with someone else had been torture. Dancing with her had been perfect. No matter what the music, she fit his body like they had been dancing together forever.

"I am so fucking sorry I do not get drunk every time I turn around," she hissed at him. Cliff assumed she was pissed because she had been found out.

"Maybe getting drunk will loosen you up because the uptight bitch attitude gets old fast." He saw her flinch at his words. It was exactly the reaction he wanted until he saw the pain in her face. Then he wanted to take it back.

"You don't think I want to drink? That I don't want to go out with my sisters every chance I can? That I miss a lot by staying away from it? If that makes me an uptight bitch, then I guess I am." She turned from him and walked through the mass of people toward the door. Before she disappeared into the crowd, he set his drink down and followed her.

Once they made it to the open door and out onto the sidewalk, he yelled because she wasn't stopping. "Then do it, Mabel. Get smashed! What's the worst that will happen?"

Spinning around, she yelled right back, "I will die!"

"Being a little dramatic, Mabel Lucie?" He smirked at her over-the-top answer, so much like Lucy that it was weird.

"Yeah, I guess it is. I mean, I was only in a coma for two days. That *is* a bit dramatic," she called over her shoulder as she took off on a jog away from him.

Cliff ran to catch up with her quickly and grabbed her arm. The fact that he had almost lost her before he even knew her was scary. When she had stopped fighting his grip, he asked, "When?"

"It doesn't matter. You'll just blab to Lucy." She tried to jerk her arm from him, but he held on. He knew he should let her go but was suddenly afraid to lose her.

"I won't, I promise." He made an X on his chest with his free hand.

"Just forget I said anything." The pain in her eyes said she didn't believe him, didn't want him to know anything more. It was that pain that loosened his grip, and she succeeded in pulling her arm away from his grasp. Instantly, she took off at a run toward the ocean.

Cliff let her run. He knew he could run longer than she could, so he let her go. Soon enough, she started to slow and then walk until she finally stopped under the lights from the bar far off in the distance. Cliff stood back and let her have a moment to herself. His mind was racing. Had Lucy ever said anything about Mabel and alcohol? He knew she hadn't because she made fun of Mabel's teetotaling ways.

Mabel sank to the sand so close to the waterline, letting the waves wash over her feet every time the surf came in. "Go away, Cliff."

He ignored her words and walked up behind her, sinking into the sand and putting his arms around her. He waited for her to push him away, but instead, she just leaned into his chest. Her breathing was still heavy from the run, or maybe because she was crying, he didn't know. It didn't matter; he wasn't letting her go.

"Tell me, Maby." He kissed her neck because it was exposed, and he couldn't stop himself. She almost died, and he wouldn't have ever known the feeling of her being in his arms.

"Nothing to tell," she whispered to the ocean.

"Please," he begged, pulling her closer as he shifted so that she was trapped between his legs.

"Nobody knows. I don't want them to."

"I won't tell. I'll take it to my grave."

They sat in silence for a long time, watching the waves that were barely visible in the darkness. The surf rushed over their feet before flowing back to the sea.

"I used to drink like Lucy, probably more. You know how Sera is; she let us do our thing. Freshman year of college was when I really got into binge drinking. All week I would study, and on Friday and Saturday, I wasn't sober at all. Sunday was my recovery day. After a few months, my grades started to slip, but I didn't want to change. I was having fun. Then I dated this guy for a few weeks, and he introduced me to speed." Her voice was husky as she took a ragged breath.

"I dumped him but kept using speed for over a year. I was on it all the time. It made college easy. I didn't need to sleep anymore. There was more time to study and more time to party. After finals in the middle of my sophomore year, I celebrated by going to a big party just off campus. Nothing new; I had done it many, many times by then. It was my life. But that night, I passed out in the hallway of my dorm. When I woke up, I was in the hospital, and it was two days later. I had gone into an alcohol-induced coma, and I could have easily died. Too easily."

"Why wasn't your mom called?" He kissed her neck again. Sera would have been there for her, no matter what Maby had done. These girls had gotten the best stepmom a kid could ask for her, and as far as he knew, she had never judged a single one of them.

"Dad was my emergency contact because he was still oddly on staff with the university, but he never came." She shrugged. The Lovely girls' dad didn't care for his kids at all. He had walked away when they were young and never came back. Most of them couldn't even remember him.

"You were alone?"

"Lucy was working two jobs, Harper was in France, and the other two were in high school. It went under the radar, so nobody ever knew. But the doctor told me that if I did it again, I would die. I was lucky enough that time to wake up; next time, I won't be so lucky. I shouldn't drink at all." She leaned back into him as the water ran over their bodies.

"Wasn't it the speed that was the issue?" he asked.

"When I drink, I usually crave it. The buzz isn't the same without the high. I know if I drink enough, I'll find some. I'm an addict ... and far from perfect." She repeated the words that he had accused her of being.

"You're perfect to me. Addict or not." He pulled her body closer to him, not wanting to let her go.

"When did you know it was me?" she asked.

"When I called Lucy to see what kind of donut she wanted. She apologized for missing our flight."

"I pulled it off yesterday?" He could feel her giggle more than hear it as she spoke, glad her mood was changing.

"Yes, you did, perfect Mabel." He lightly kissed her neck again because he couldn't stop himself. The smell of Mabel and the salty, briny water was intoxicating.

"I thought I did pretty good today. I mean, parasailing? Lucy would have hated that, but I nailed it." He felt her giggle again.

"You did, and the nude beach—she would have hated that too." Cliff reluctantly pulled away from her and got to his feet.

"I know. She's way more conservative than I am." Her hand slipped into his so he could pull her to her feet.

"You? You were comfortable naked?" He kept her hand as they walked toward the light of the bar.

"Way more than Lucy is. Lucy can be a prude when she's sober. I got suspended twice in school for streaking." Her words surprised him. He never thought she broke the rules, even if she was a Lovely sister. Somehow, he always put her in a different category than the others, but she was the same in so many ways.

"I wish I had known that. I thought you would've run away from that beach in horror," he admitted as they passed the bar, heading for the hotel. The night was over, and he was with Mabel tonight, not Lucy. No more pretending one was the other.

"I think I'm a little more Lucy sometimes than Lucy is."

"Maybe sometimes Lucy is more Mabel than Lucy," Cliff countered. He unlocked their room.

Once inside the room, they ran out of things to say. The silence was strained and awkward. All he could think about was how wet they both were and how they needed to get their wet clothes off. Then, there was the bed that filled up the room. The thought of sharing that bed with her again ... he knew he wouldn't be able to keep his hands off her this time.

Without a word, she went into the bathroom, and he heard the shower come on. He wanted to join her but controlled his urge because it was Mabel, and he'd had sex with Lucy once. And now he wanted to have sex with Mabel? That was a line he shouldn't even be thinking about crossing, but he couldn't seem to stop.

Pulling out his phone, he left the hotel room and dialed a familiar number. Of course, she answered on the second ring, breathless and happy to hear from him.

"Cliff, how's your vacation going? I bet it's warm down there. It's muggy here today. I wish I was at the beach," Lucy said without taking a breath.

"It's very nice down here," he admitted.

"Did Kevin and Beth go?"

"Yeah, they're here, but I've been ignoring them." He didn't want to reveal that Mabel was with him because then he would have to explain a lot.

"Good. He's an ass. Before you left, he stayed in my room and he tried to hook up with me. Cheat on Beth with me. What a turn around. Jerk," Lucy stated blithely.

"I hope you stop taking him home."

"He followed me. But yes, I'm completely over him," Lucy replied, but Cliff wasn't a hundred percent sure of her words. He'd heard them too often before.

"Hey, have you ever thought about us as a couple?" he asked, needing to know the answer. "I mean, Kevin and Beth hooked up…. Have you ever thought about us?"

"God, no," she said quickly, then added, "Have you?"

"No, I mean, we've never been attracted to each other, right?" All he needed was her to hint about the night they hooked up. Just something that said she remembered something and that him thinking the thoughts he was thinking about with Mabel were wrong.

"Are you even a guy, Cliff?" she asked with a laugh.

"Not to you, Luce," he said, knowing she still didn't remember that night. But could he forget it if he slept with her sister? Would he be forever comparing them?

"I have to go. Harper and I are going out tonight. Maby's still missing, but she should surface soon. Maby's never been good at hiding things from me, including herself," Lucy said, but Cliff knew her sister had secrets she never wanted Lucy to know.

"Have fun and miss me," he said.

"I will," she replied and hung up on him.

Back in the hotel room, Mabel was in bed, so he slipped into the bathroom to shower off the sand from sitting in the surf. It only took a few minutes, and he was climbing into bed with her.

Today he should have found another hotel room because tonight, they both knew who the other was. That, and he couldn't trust himself around this woman. All he wanted to do was touch her, hold her, and do everything his mind had been dreaming of since the airport.

"Goodnight, Cliff." She was facing away from him.

"Goodnight, Maby. Or do I have to call you Mabel Lucie?" He lay on his back, looking at the ceiling. Her sisters all called her Maby, but not a lot of other people did that he knew about. Did they use both her first names? He had no idea.

"Miss Lovely is fine. I mean, we barely know each other," she said, but he didn't even think she believed that anymore. They knew a lot about each other after just one day. Which might be why she added quietly, "Maby."

"Goodnight, Maby." He looked at her back. She was so close that he could touch her, but he didn't dare.

She then shifted in bed until she could look at him, getting even closer to him. "Do you really think there's nothing that can be done to help Lucy with her reading?" Her head rested on her hand, and her elbow was on the pillow.

"There is, but she will never do it. And now she has her catering business and doesn't need it so much. She lets Harper deal with the contracts and such. She's really found a way to make her life work." He had been surprised that it had happened, that in the last year, she'd been able to make her life work seamlessly around her disability.

"But I don't want her to struggle through life. I want to help her," Mabel admitted. She loved her sister and didn't want her to have difficulties.

"There's nothing you can do, Maby. It's up to Lucy." He wanted to pull her into his arms and make her pain go away.

She must have agreed because her head went back to the pillow, but she continued to look into his eyes.

In the near darkness, he looked at her, unable to touch because he knew he wouldn't stop if he did. He just looked his fill, but it wasn't enough anymore. Over the last day, he had gotten to know Maby Lovely, and she wasn't the woman he had always thought that she was. She had her reasons for being reserved, and they had nothing to do with trying to be different than her twin or her other sisters. It was because of her and what she had faced in life.

"Do you ever do something on vacation that you would never do in real life?" Maby asked, almost in a whisper.

"Like what?" He held his breath—was it possible she felt it too? Could it be that he wasn't alone in this?

"Like playing tennis every day, but when you get back home, you don't even think about playing tennis again. You just go back to how you were before you played tennis, never thinking about doing it again." Gently, she placed her hand on his chest.

"I don't think I can play tennis when we get back, because fuck, I want to play tennis with you." He ran his hand up her arm, across her shoulder, and into her chocolate hair, pulling her mouth to his.

Willingly, she let him lead her there. They were both on the same page and wanted to play tennis, but they didn't want their lives back home to change at all. He would still just be Lucy's friend, and she would be her sister. And this would be over.

His tongue slipped past her lips and tasted her sweetness, just like he had on the plane. Her body pressed closer, molding perfectly to his. Cliff ran his hand over her hair and down her back.

Pulling away slightly, a thrill ran through him as she groaned and shifted her body. He grabbed the hem of her shirt and started pulling it up, needing to see her again. Today at the beach hadn't been enough; he needed to touch, to taste. To memorize everything about it.

Once the shirt was off, he cupped the breasts he had watched in the sun today. They were warm and full, and he knew he had to taste them to see if they tasted of salt still or if her shower had washed that off. Dipping his head, she arched her back so he could take her beaded nipple into his mouth. No salt, but just the taste of Mabel was still amazing.

Her fingers were in his hair, holding him to her breast as she leaned back. The movement pushed her breast tighter to him. Her hands slid over his body, driving him crazy.

Moving across to her other nipple, she rolled him onto his back so that she was leaning over him to rub her satin-clad core over his hard cock.

"Maby," he groaned at her slow movements.

She did it again. "You like that, Cliff?"

"Do you even have to ask, Maby?" His hands slid over her ass and ripped the satin away from her body. Then trailed them down between her legs and ran a single finger over her wet clit as she continued to slide up and down his length.

"Just want to make sure you're enjoying playing tennis," she hissed the last word as his fingers hit the perfect spot and rubbed.

He watched her let go of control as an orgasm made her moan his name, and her hip's slow movement ceased completely until she was just grinding her core into his cock. Watching her in the dim light as she regained her breath, he sat up and kissed her neck and breasts.

"You're beautiful, Maby," he whispered, trying to taste and touch as much of her as possible.

"Do you know what I like about tennis, Cliff?" Mabel asked when she could finally breathe again.

"What?" He lazily ran his hand over her stomach to her breasts.

"How fast it is." She giggled and looped her fingers into the waistband of his boxers.

"Mostly, it goes slow," he said in confusion as he lifted his hips, letting her remove the clothing.

"Not when I play it." She pressed him back into the mattress.

Letting her take the lead, she straddled him, and he slid into her hot, wet body. She set the rhythm until he couldn't take it any longer and rolled them over so that she was on her back. Grabbing her hips, his thrusts increased and intensified. She moved with him, gasping with each thrust until her body was gripping his as another orgasm rolled through her body, taking him along with her.

Cliff collapsed beside her. he didn't even have the breath to speak. Tucking her into his arms, he kissed the top of her head. He already knew he was going to be in trouble when this vacation was over.

He was starting to really like tennis.

CHAPTER THIRTEEN

"WHERE ARE YOU GOING?" Mabel's eyes were barely open as she watched him pull on his shorts, covering his amazing body that she already wanted to touch again. This vacation was going to be too short. Way too short.

"For a run. Want to come with?" He grinned at her. Fuck, he had a sexy grin.

Mabel tried to pinpoint the moment she had started to think Cliff was sexy, but she couldn't because he had always been sexy to her. For over a year, she had been avoiding him when he was in the house because she knew she could like him. But his life and hers were completely opposite. His lack of ambition made him unacceptable. But on vacation, he was perfect, and she would enjoy him until the plane ride home.

"Yes." She surprised herself; it had been years since she went for a run, and she had hated it then. But him just saying it made it sound fun. He made everything fun.

"Get moving then." He walked over to the bed and pulled her out by the hand. His eyes running over her body as the blankets fell away, as she was still completely naked.

"Are you sure you want to run?" Her eyes drifted to his running shorts, where the evidence was clear that he had other things on his mind.

"Don't tempt me, Lovely." He pulled her close and ran his lips over her forehead and then let her go.

Grabbing her bag, she went into the bathroom to change into an outfit that she could run in. As quickly as she could, she left the bathroom and grabbed the tennis shoes she had worn on the plane trip. They weren't ideal for actual running, but way better than the sandals she had worn all day yesterday.

Within minutes, she was following him, realizing she had made a big mistake. Mabel knew she couldn't call herself a runner, and now she didn't think she ever would. Running wasn't fun.

Cliff kept circling back to make sure she was okay, but her pace slowed with each passing block until she was just walking, and not very fast.

Running up to her, he turned and started to walk backward, looking at her. "Tired, Maby?"

"Not a runner. You go; I'll be around here when you get done," she admitted.

"We can't get breakfast down the path if you aren't there."

"You run and get it and bring it back to me." She grinned at her pun.

"I don't know what you like."

"I'll eat about anything."

"No, you won't. You don't like lemon or fish." He reminded her of the meals he had ordered for her the day before—the ones she thought he hadn't noticed she didn't like.

"I have to admit I don't enjoy lemon donuts, but if you choose anything with chocolate, you'll be okay in my book Better than okay, actually. I'll be around here, enjoying my time with the ocean." She waved her hand at the scenery.

"Are you sure, Lovely? I'd hate to have to explain how you were kidnapped in Florida while staying with friends in Minnesota."

"I will lie to my family if I want to, Cliff!" she stated, hating that she was lying to them. But this time away was exactly what she had needed.

"You do you, Maby." He pulled her into his arms and kissed her because they were on vacation and still could.

Her toes curled in the tennis shoes that were making her feet hot as her body was pressed nicely to his sweaty one. Quietly, she whimpered when he pushed her away, missing his touch immediately. She was enjoying this vacation *way* more than she ever should.

"I'll bring us back something. You stay here or go back to the hotel; I'll find you," he promised and took off.

She watched him run away from her until he was gone. Until this week, she had never known he was a runner or exercised in general. She'd thought he was a huge lush, but nothing else. But at this point, Mabel realized that beyond him being Lucy's friend, she knew very little about him. He hadn't gone to the same high school the sisters had gone to.

One day, he became friends with Lucy, and suddenly, he was working at the Grog all the time. Or so she heard. She didn't go in there a lot since she stayed away from situations that would make her drink too much. Unless invited out by her sisters, she didn't go, and sometimes not even then.

But he was close to her age, and he worked as a bartender. There had to be more to him than that. At this point, she didn't know if she wanted to know or not—this wasn't a relationship. Whatever they were doing had an expiration date, and it was tomorrow afternoon. Four short days from beginning to end, with two plane rides included. Not enough time in her book.

She made her way toward the beach, stepping into the loose sand and pulling off her shoes and socks to enjoy the feel. Soon they would be back home.

As she dipped her toes into the cool water, her phone went off in her pocket. Absently she pulled it out and looked at the screen. Lucy. But she wasn't in the mood to talk with her sister yet, but it wasn't for the same reason she had yesterday. Now she didn't want her twin to interfere with her vacation from reality.

As it rang again, Mabel put that thought aside. If she couldn't face her sister now, would she be able to later? The rift between them was big and seemed to be growing bigger every day. It was time to close that up.

"What?" she said harshly, even though it wasn't what she was feeling.

"Where are you? I've called everyone you know." Lucy accused her.

"I doubt that, Lucy." Since she mostly hung out with her sisters and people from work, and Lucy didn't know any of them.

"Okay, maybe not. But only because I don't know any of your friends' numbers. Can we have lunch today?" Lucy's voice was tentative.

"No, I just need more time."

"I didn't sleep with him. You know that, right? I'm not that big of a slut." Lucy insisted, and Mabel heard the tremor in her voice. Was she going to cry?

"He's my boss, and I have to work with him all the time. My coworkers think something happened." Mabel laid out her evidence, no longer on the defensive about it. She wanted Lucy to explain what happened.

"It was just a dance, one. Yesterday I went to your work and talked to the guy across the hallway from your office. He said that guy was almost stalking you last year. You need to report that, Maby," Lucy said. Mabel knew she should have, but she hadn't wanted to make waves when she first was starting at her new job.

"You don't understand, Lucy," Mabel replied, dismissing her advice. But she knew her sister hadn't done anything wrong except dance with the wrong guy. Now Mabel felt guilty about taking her sister's vacation. She should have just stayed at home and talked to Lucy.

"I guess I don't. I've never been to college." Lucy's voice was tinged with a sadness that Mabel hadn't ever caught before.

"You could have gone to college." Mabel kicked at the sand with her toe.

Lucy laughed in her ear. "Me and college? Right. You know better than anyone, I would never have lasted a day in college."

"But did you want to?"

There was silence on the other end. Was her sister not going to answer? Not once had she said anything about college when they were in high school. It hadn't really been an option with her grades. "Yeah, I wanted to. I wanted to go with you; we're twins."

"We still are."

"It's different now. We aren't as close as when we were twins." Lucy's words made Mabel wonder when her sister thought they had stopped being twins, because no matter what, they were still twins and would be forever.

"We live together," she reminded Lucy.

"But we never do anything together. Ever."

"We should. We should do something soon."

"Today, lunch," Lucy stated again.

"No, I'm busy." Mabel looked out over the ocean.

"Okay, when you aren't busy, we will. Maybe we can go out for drinks. Agatha's starting at a jazz bar next week. We can go watch her get fired." Lucy chuckled. Their little sister had a tendency to not work very long at any one place.

"Find out when she's working, and we'll go," Mabel promised her sister. She wanted to talk to her twin now more than ever.

"Okay, but tell me you're not mad at me still," Lucy whined.

"Maybe just a little, but I'm starting to get over it now," she said as she watched the water lap at the sand.

"See you soon?"

"Yes, soon," Mabel said and hung up on her sister. Tomorrow all this would end. She and Cliff would head back to their real lives. Back to where they were not sleeping together.

After spending one day with Cliff, she was enjoying their time together so much that she wasn't excited to go back to where he was just her sister's best friend. Right now, he was just a mile or so down the beach, but she missed him. She wanted him back as soon as she could get him. But after tomorrow, they were going to be apart forever.

CHAPTER FOURTEEN

His morning run was shorter than it usually was because he wanted to get back to Mabel as soon as possible. Not that he was actually worried something would happen to her, but because he had started to miss her the moment he'd left her behind.

After getting two chocolate donuts from the same shop he had purchased them from the day before, he headed back toward her. Cliff wanted to spend the entire day with her, and this time without her pretending to be Lucy. Today she was going to be one hundred percent Mabel.

Sadly, he wouldn't get to spend the entire day with her because today, he had to go and visit his grandmother for a few hours. He came down to Florida every year, where she had retired to escape from the cold. Since his father rarely made it down to see his mother, Cliff made sure he got in one trip a year to see her. Each visit they had bonded over their joint dislike of his father. Over the years, he had wondered if his mom ever came to visit the woman for the same reason.

Originally, he had planned to just leave Lucy, Kevin, and Beth at the hotel and pretend he was hooking up with someone. But since he was with Mabel, and the fact that they were hooking up, was going to make it impossible for him to go alone. He actually wanted to tell her the truth, which was a shock to him. Nobody knew about his family.

Making his way back to the spot where he had left her, he was surprised to find that she hadn't gone far. Mabel was still sitting in the sand, looking out into the ocean. Today she didn't even remind him of Lucy, not one bit.

His eyes were on the curve of her back as her chin rested on her knees. She must have felt him near because she turned to him with a smile on her face.

"How was your run?"

"Good," was all he could say. She took his breath away.

"I doubt that; it was a run. But maybe breakfast will be." She grabbed the bag from his hands.

"We have to get back to the hotel." He grabbed her arm.

She scrambled to her feet in alarm, almost dropping the bag. Her smile was completely gone. "Has something happened? My family?"

Stopping at her reaction, he pulled her close to him. "No, I just need you right now, way more than a chocolate donut."

Her instant laugh made his heart pound. When she let go, she was gorgeous. At this point, he wanted to say screw the world so he could keep her forever.

"I think we're on the same page, Cliff." Pulling out of his arms, she took his hand and led the way back to their hotel room.

Three hours later, they were back on the beach, both happy and relaxed. Just what they both needed. Mabel was laying on her stomach, letting the sun warm her back as Cliff sat next to her, unable to stop touching her exposed skin.

"Would you be upset if I left you alone for a few hours today?" He ran a finger down her spine until it hit the top of her bikini bottoms, then followed that.

"That's okay," she said just above a whisper.

"If you don't want me to go, I am fine with that." He followed the line of her bikini bottom until he went up her side making her sigh.

"If you have something to do, do it. I'll be fine. Maybe get some reading done. I haven't read at all since I got here."

"I should visit my grandma while I'm here, but I won't if you need me here."

"Cliff, go visit your grandma. She's probably excited to see you."

"I hate to leave you alone." He kissed her lower back.

"I'll be fine," Mabel said.

"When you pretended to be Lucy and were naked, did you remember you had a tattoo?" He traced it with his fingers.

"Shit." She sat up as if it just dawned on her that she had it. "I forgot."

"It's adorable. You have your name on you." He pulled her onto his lap.

"I just like the author's signature. Is that a crime?"

"Yes, it is. Now for your punishment." He started lightly biting her neck and making her laugh.

"Stop it, Cliff." She pushed him as she continued to laugh.

"I have to take you back to the hotel. Grandma will have to wait." He started to get up and pull her with him.

"No, Cliff. You have to go see her. I'll be here when you get back." She pushed him away from her.

"But I want to stay with you," he protested, trying to pull her back into his arms.

"No. Grandma time. Go get changed to see her." Mabel pushed him toward the room.

"You should come with." The words were out of his mouth before he could stop them. No way was their relationship in a place where she should introduce her to his grandma. Plus, his grandma would never not talk about money. It was her favorite topic.

"I, um, have no idea what to say. We aren't a couple or anything," she said stopping to sit on a chair.

"We can pretend. I see her a few times a year, and she never talks to my dad. She probably won't even remember you once we leave." It was a lie; the woman was sharp as a tack and was always begging him to get married and give her grandkids.

"Thanks, sounds like she won't like me."

"She will love you, I swear. She just doesn't remember everything all the time anymore."

"You can just go alone. I will wait here for you."

"Nope, you are going to meet my grandma and then we can get some takeout and come back here. It will be fun." He smiled at her, hoping she would just agree with him because he wasn't leaving her alone until the plane landed tomorrow. With just twenty-four hours left on this relationship, he wasn't wasting any of it.

With coxing and promises for later, he got her out of her swimsuit and into shorts and a T-shirt for the trip to see Grandma. Though she wasn't actually happy about going with him, she was doing it.

"Do you ever see your grandparents?" he asked as they drove across town. Lucy had never talked about any family besides her sisters and Sera.

"No, we don't have any. Well, we must, but neither Bradford nor Judith were too interested in them, and I have no idea where or who they are. Sera has parents, but I have never met them," she said. Cliff had always found it odd that the sisters always called their birth parents by their given names. If any of them said "mom," it was in reference to their stepmom, Sera. Lately, "dad" was her fiancé, Harrison, who hated being called dad by the five older girls.

"Not one? I have just my grandma now. Mom's parents are gone, and Grandpa has been gone since before I was born." The small family had been annoying when he was younger, but now it was just how it was. Had he wanted siblings and aunts and uncles? Yes, but he was used to it now.

"I guess I never think about it. They've just never been there. Extended family wasn't a tradition I ever had." She shrugged.

"Do you wish you had?"

"Of course. I also wish my parents cared about us and never left us, and we were a big traditional family. But in reality, I wouldn't trade Sera raising us for anything. And now I'm getting a dad, so things will change." She smiled when she said dad because it was in jest.

"Do you like your new dad?" he asked. Lucy was happy for Sera to find love, but he didn't know if Mabel was.

"What's not to like? He's madly in love with Sera, and he loves us all equally." She folded her arms.

"He loves his two kids and tolerates the rest of you," Cliff stated, which was the truth. Harrison Dean didn't dislike his future step-daughters, but as a unit, they were a lot.

"*Equally*. And he lets Sera be herself. So far, he hasn't even pushed her to move in with him."

"He talks about it all the time," Cliff reminded her. He had heard him say it on numerous occasions.

"He does, but so far, he hasn't demanded anything. I think she's easing everyone into the change. I mean, she should move the two little ones out, and the rest of us will survive. But she's weaning us."

"Do you need weaning?"

"Yes. We fight and bicker and yell, but in the end, we all like to be at home. It's nice that we're close. But if any of us actually move out, what then? So, we stay."

"The house is literally packed, Maby. Add a man or two, and it's overflowing."

"You would be surprised how many times it is almost completely empty. The silence is defining."

"Here we are. This is where Grandma Scott lives." He pointed to it, hoping she would think it was more of a retirement home and not her house. could the place looked like a fancy, multi-unit development and not just one home.

"Nice. Does she like it down here?" Mabel leaned forward to look at the top floors as he parked.

"Yeah, she hated winter, and now she doesn't have to deal with it," he said, though he had never really asked the woman. She seemed as happy here as she had been in Minnesota.

After parking, he helped her out of the car and held her hand as they walked up the sidewalk to the front door, which opened as they approached. "Good afternoon, Mr. Scott."

Cliff looked at his grandmother's aging butler, Nigel. The man had worked for the woman since before Cliff was born, and still he was just as formal with him as ever.

"Hi, Nigel. is Grandmother here?" he asked, knowing he had been waiting for them.

"Yes, in the Florida room." Nigel led them through the house. It was as formal and stuffy as always; Cliff hated it.

"Not what I was picturing," Mabel whispered from beside him, her hand clenching his tightly.

"I should have warned you." He knew he should have but hadn't wanted to.

His family had money, but it had nothing to do with him as a person now. Years ago, he had stepped away from it and was happy for it. Making his own way. People liked him for him, not for being Cliff Scott V.

Which was why he shouldn't have taken Mabel with him. He hoped she wouldn't change how she looked at him because she was here.

"Yup," she said as they entered the Florida room, which faced the open water of the Gulf.

Barbara Scott was reading a novel on the love seat, or pretending to, so she wouldn't look like she had been waiting for his arrival. Just like Nigel pretending he hadn't been waiting for his knock on the door.

"Hello, Grandma," Cliff said as she tossed the book down and jumped to her feet.

"Clifton! You came." He accepted her hug, dropping Mabel's hand.

"I told you I would." He didn't look at Mabel, who knew how much he had been trying to get out of it.

"Well, I sometimes don't know with you," she answered and pushed him from her arms and grabbed his cheeks in her hands. "Look at you! You are looking more and more like my Clifton every day."

"I don't know," Cliff argued.

"Oh, yes. We were married by the time we were your age. Hell, we had already had Cliffy by then. Cliffy." She sighed at the word. "What an asshole."

"Grandma!"

"Well, I just call them like I see them. The only good thing to come from that kid was you, and of course, Jeannie," Barbara said.

"Jeannie is my mother," Cliff explained to Mabel.

His words brought the older woman's attention right to her. "Cliff, you brought me a woman! Are you going to marry her? Do I know her?"

"Settle down, Grandma. This is Maby Lovely."

Barbara looked Mabel up and down and smiled. "No, Cliff, she *is* lovely. A woman likes to hear it sometimes."

"Sorry, ma'am." Mabel laughed. "Maby is my nickname. My full name is Mabel Lucie Lovely."

"I don't know any Lovelys. Do I know any Lovelys?" Barbara asked Mabel as if she might answer.

"I don't know, but I have quite a few sisters," Mabel told her.

"You don't know any, Grandma. Her family isn't from money." Cliff hated to say the words. He would take the Lovely family over money any day of the week.

His words earned him a scowl from Mabel, but then she nodded in agreement, letting it go. Money wasn't something that any of the Lovely's were interested in. Except Harper.

"Does your father know about her?" Barbara smirked and looked over Mabel.

"No." Was all he said, and the man never would if Cliff had his way.

"I'll pay you big money to tell him." Barbara grinned and looked Mabel up and down again like a prized horse. Apparently, telling his dad would piss him off.

"Grandma, she's a college professor. Dad won't care." His own stepmom was a few years older than Cliff and had been a ditzy waitress before she got married.

"Oh, he'll care. What do you teach, Mabel Lucie Lovely?" Barb took Mabel by the hand and led her to the couch she had been sitting on earlier.

"Children's literature," Mabel answered, her eyes taking in the room.

"I don't like it, Clifton. You need a floozy on your arm. Cliffy would hate that." Barbara turned away from Mabel again.

"My father isn't afraid of dating floozies. Also, I am not dating someone just to make my dad mad." Which was why he didn't date. Period.

"I'll pay good money for you to do just that." Barbara jumped to her feet, leaving Mabel on the couch.

"Nope, I'm keeping Maby." Suddenly, he wished he could keep her forever. Except they had agreed their relationship would only last a short time.

"Too bad. No offence, young lady, but his dad would probably approve of you." Barbara turned to Mabel.

Mabel smiled at Barbara for a moment. "I'm sorry I'm such a good catch."

"Educated!" Barbara threw her hands in the air.

"Sorry, Mrs. Scott." Mabel said again, leaned back against the cushions and rolled her eyes, relaxing finally.

"Just call me Babs. I'll let Cliffy's new wife be Mrs. Scott. I did that for too many years." Barbara started sit again.

"How long where you married to Cliff's grandfather?" Mabel asked.

"Seven of the longest years of my life, dear." Barbara made it sound like it was a century.

"I expected longer," Mable mumbled.

"Oh, sweetie. He married me for money, and I married him to piss off my father. It all worked out," Barbara explained it away as if that was exactly why everyone got married.

"You never remarried?" Mabel asked in disbelief.

"Of course not! I don't need a man to be happy." Barbara tapped her leg.

"More to the point, she never found anyone else willing to put up with her," Cliff provided the real answer.

At Cliff's words, his grandmother just laughed. "If I remarried, I would lose my alimony. No way am I letting Clifton off that easily."

CHAPTER FIFTEEN

FISH HAD BEEN on the menu until Cliff told Nigel that Mabel didn't like it. Then suddenly, it was beef. The large table was set for three but held more dishes than her family of eight usually used for a meal. Not that Mabel was noticing. All she could see was that Cliff had lied to her. Lied to everyone. He came from money. Not that he had actually said differently, but it was still a lie by omission.

Not even just money, but super money. The kind of money where money is never even thought of. Though Cliff didn't seem to notice the house full of expensive things, she did.

Which left her wondering what Cliff was up to. He was a bartender who practically lived with Lucy at their house. Though she had never heard him complain about money, or even talk about it, she had always assumed he had very little of it.

But there was no way the grandson of this lady was living in poverty. This woman exuded wealth. After all, she was a Scott, something she kept repeating.

By the time she and Cliff were saying goodbye, with hugs and odd envelopes of cash, the two were on their way back to the hotel. As Cliff drove, Mabel tentatively opened the envelope and looked inside.

"Why did she give me money?" She looked at the bills. It was what she expected but still didn't believe the woman had just given her cash.

"Grandma shows her love with cash." Cliff didn't seem bothered by it as he drove through the streets, his own envelope in his pocket. It had his name written on it and was thicker than her own plain envelope.

Before the envelopes, she had started to like Cliff's grandma. She was spunky and had some great stories about her life. And even a few ones about Cliff when he was little and an uncontrollable kid. It seemed he hadn't quite outgrown that.

"You should at least say no," she said, not knowing what to even do with the money. It seemed like a lot.

"That would hurt her feelings. You can't hurt her feelings." He turned his pouty eyes on her, the ones that she hated. They were what he used on everyone when he was in trouble. Not that he was in trouble this time—it was his grandma who had given them the cash.

"Do you just come down here for the cash?" She had to ask. His answer would change everything about how she viewed the past few days.

"No, I come to see her. The cash is just a bonus. A much-needed bonus that keeps a roof over my head and food in my stomach." He patted his belly.

"Nice try, Cliff. Don't think I don't see you for who you are. You are slumming—a poor rich kid who's slumming. You come from more money than god, and you've split a drinking tab with me during this trip. I had to pay the cover to get into that bar the first night because you were out of cash!" She waved the envelope at him.

"I *was* out of cash, but I did get more from the ATM yesterday. Did you notice that?" He didn't turn away from the traffic as he said it.

"No more ATMs for a while." She tossed the envelope on his lap. She'd loved the time she had spent with his grandmother and didn't need to be paid for it. In fact, she would happily do it again for free.

"I love her, Mabel. I can't help if she gives me money. I visit my mom, and she doesn't give me money. Can we just drop it? I don't like that I'm from money. I don't usually use it. I make my own way." His jaw was set in a look she hadn't glimpsed before. Cliff was mad.

"With a little help." She pointed to the envelope.

"Sometimes," he admitted with a shrug.

"So, Grandma hates your dad?" Mabel stated the obvious. The woman couldn't say a good thing about the man all afternoon.

"Yes, when Dad started to work for Grandpa, they became estranged and never got close again. I understand her feelings. Dad is a jerk."

"But your mom is okay?"

"My mom is great. She mostly raised me on her own. Dad had no time for children, I'm closer to her side of the family, though there aren't many anymore. And Grandma. Like you, my family is small," Cliff said.

Mabel knew that his family was nothing like her family. They were completely different and most likely couldn't relate to each other. But after seeing how Cliff was raised, she wondered why he enjoyed spending time with her family. Why did sitting at her house with her sisters watching TV all day appeal to a man who could buy anything, do anything? Except he always appeared to be neither, just a guy living the life of a poor bartender who liked to have a good time.

"So, what's the plan for the rest of the day?" she asked, wanting to change the topic from his extreme wealth to less heavy things.

"My plan, Mabel Lucie, is to take you to bed and not get out until the plane leaves tomorrow. Got an issue with that?" His eyes were on her, and with just that look, she was ready to jump him.

Luckily, he was pulling into the parking lot of their hotel, so she didn't have to wait long.

"Not a single one," she said as she got out of the car the moment it stopped.

Cliff got out and raced for her, swooping her into his arms and carrying her into the dive hotel. His strong arms held her close, and their eyes met as she wrapped her arms around his neck. That is until he nearly tripped, and she screamed and clung to him tighter.

The scream must have been louder than she thought because the door to the room beside theirs opened, and Beth looked out at them. Instantly, she glared at them and said something to the room behind her.

Before Cliff could take another step, Kevin leaned out of the room and paled at the sight of Mabel—who he thought was Lucy—in Cliff's arms.

Without a thought, Mabel turned to Cliff and kissed him exactly like she wanted to, giving Kevin a show. Cliff either went with her on it or had simply wanted to kiss her as much as she wanted to kiss him.

"Get a room," Kevin called to them.

Cliff stopped kissing her and called back, "We have one and plan to use it extensively. Just like we have been doing since we got here. How about you, Kev? Is Beth satisfied? She doesn't look it."

"She has nothing to complain about."

"I think she does," Mabel said as Cliff dropped her to her feet. "Since I've been with you both, I find your performance and stamina a bit lacking in comparison." His arms tightened around her shoulders as they started walking toward the door again.

"That's not true, Lucy." Beth jumped in. Kevin smiled and pulled her to him, and the woman actually melted into his arms. Gross.

"Come on, Beth, you can't expect me to believe that you think Kevin is better in bed than Cliff?" Mabel asked.

"He is. With Cliff, it sometimes just last so long. I got tired of it," Beth stated.

"And the faking of orgasms gets tiring too," Mable commiserated.

"It does." Beth sighed and then realized she'd said it out loud.

Before she could say anything else, Cliff pushed her into the hotel room and slammed the door shut. With a laugh, Cliff grabbed her shirt and pulled Mabel close as he leaned against the door. "You are pure evil, Mabel Lucie Lovely."

"An evil genius, you mean." She ran her hands under his shirt, ready to strip him down now that they were alone.

"That is exactly what I meant." He let her go, but only to grab her up in his arms and carry her to the bed. "An evil genius and all mine until tomorrow. How are we going to pass the time?"

"I think making so much noise having sex that they both regret breaking it off with us." She decided to get things moving by taking off her own shirt and throwing it at the wall that separated their rooms.

"Except you never dated Kevin." He did the same with his.

"He doesn't know that. And he never will." She shimmied out of her shorts and did it again, only to miss.

"You are sexier right now than ever before." He pulled off her sandal, and it hit the wall, followed by her second one.

"Are you attracted to my mind, Mr. Scott?" She peeled off his shorts, letting them fall to the floor, forgetting about making noise.

"I'm attracted to anything that is Maby Lovely right now." His hands ran up her bare legs and then slid her panties from her body, his eyes in her skin as it was revealed.

"Then make me scream, Cliff." Just him looking at her made her pant.

"My pleasure, Maby." His hands spread her legs as his lips kissed up her inner thigh until she was screaming his name, and it wasn't for anyone but her and Cliff. He was all she was thinking about.

CHAPTER SIXTEEN

BESIDE HIM, Mabel slouched down into a chair and ate a bag of chips, loudly. The woman had been eating nonstop since they had gotten to the airport. Besides the bag of chips, she had eaten a bag of candy, a candy bar, a huge brownie from the snack place, a sandwich, and now the chips.

"What?" she said between crunches.

"Nothing," he replied, full from his own sandwich. He had thought when he had bought them each one that she would've been full too.

"You forgot to feed me for almost twenty-four hours, Cliff. I need to eat," she argued, even though she hadn't brought up her hunger until they had gotten to the airport. Before then she begged him not to leave the hotel room for any reason, so he hadn't.

For twenty-four hours, they hadn't left the hotel room, not once, instead spending hours enjoying the last moments of their vacation. Or more importantly, enjoying each other for the last time, because now that they were almost on the plane, it was over.

All they could do now was touch, at least until the plane landed. Then touching would be out also. So far, he hadn't gotten enough of her. He was starting to think he never would. The more time he got with her, the more he wanted.

Even now, he was holding her hand, so she had to eat one-handed. He brought her free hand to his lips. "If I get another chance at twenty-four hours, I won't let you eat then either."

"You say the most romantic things, Cliff. Do you want a chip?" She tilted the bag his way.

"There's only one chip I want from you, Maby," he stated huskily.

Her eyes darted to his, and she laughed. "I don't even know what that means. A chip?"

"It's all of you. There isn't one part I like more than the others."

"You make me laugh. I'm going to miss that." Her words were nearly drowned out as their flight was announced.

Pulling her up by her hand, he kissed her before saying, "You could, dare I say, spend more time with me. We could be friends." Then he grabbed their bags from the floor without letting her go.

"I think Lucy would notice if I start hanging around a lot. And you guys are always drinking. I don't want to do that." She shifted and pulled her hand from his, getting her ticket out as they got into a much shorter line than they had been in on their first flight.

"We don't always drink. I mean, we hang with your sisters and mom, we go see movies, we ..." He stopped, trying to think of times when they didn't drink. He could argue that he wasn't always to blame, that her sisters were sometimes the instigators, but he didn't think she would like to hear that.

"See? Drinking is the most of it. And I'm not going to start drinking in order to spend time with you." She handed over her ticket to the agent with a smile. He didn't have the same happiness for leaving that Mabel seemed to have.

"I'll change for you, Maby." He meant it.

"No, Cliff. Just be you. This, whatever it was, is over. We both knew that when it started." She headed into the plane, leading him to the seats in the back once again. This time, she took the window seat without talking about it.

"I'm starting to rethink the promises I made." He slid into the chair and tried to take her hand, but she busied herself with her purse and ignored him.

"Cliff. When the plane touches down, I go back to work and being me, and you go back to being you, a rich guy slumming in my house." She shut off her phone and dropped it in her bag.

"I am not slumming, Mabel. I'm just living the life I want to live." A life without the pressures of being a Scott all the time. A life without expectations he wasn't able to live up to.

"Being a drunk bartender? That's the life you want to live?" Her eyebrow raised in question.

"For now. I don't want the Scott money. I don't want the Scott responsibilities. I don't want to run a huge company, I don't want to take orders from my dad, and I never want to sit at a desk all day and ignore my family." The plane's engines roared to life below them. Soon, they'd be back to a place where they wouldn't be together anymore.

"Who are you Cliff? Where did you come from?" She leaned her head on the headrest and looked at him, her brown eyes seeming to stare right through him.

"Just humble people," he joked, but she didn't laugh.

"Who are the Scotts? I can look it up, you know. It's not like I don't know your dad's name, or your granddad's name." Cliff reassured himself that she couldn't until they landed, but that was coming fast enough.

"And Great Granddad's." He grinned at her.

"You're the fourth Clifton Scott?"

"Fifth. The fifth Cliff in a long line of them."

"What did all those Cliffs do?"

Cliff decided to give her the simplified version. "The first Clifton opened a bank, and he and his son made it huge and bought more banks and other stuff. Grandpa diversified. Now my dad just sits at a desk and watches the money come in, and I am living my best life." If she wanted to know more about his family, she could look them up.

"Bartending is the best life?" she asked again with a raised eyebrow.

"For now, it is." He shrugged. Cliff never thought about the future. He liked his present. No responsibilities, and no one to answer to but himself. Until recently, he did at least. Suddenly telling all this to Mabel made him feel selfish and spoiled.

"Don't you want to take that money and do some good? See it benefit those that might need it more then you?"

"The family trust has a charitable department, and they do a lot of good. We have the Scott name on all kinds of buildings. The new library a few miles from your house will be a Scott building." He didn't pay all that much attention to what his father did. Mostly, he tried to ignore it.

"But what about things you believe in? Things you're passionate about?" she asked, leaning toward him.

"I don't have anything like that," he argued. He didn't have a passion for anything.

"Bullshit, Cliff. What about your cousin and all the struggles he went through? There are others out there with the same issues, most without a tenth of the means you had, like Lucy. You could give to that, or work to help them. Do something to make a difference." The excitement in her eyes was almost catching, but not quite.

"Don't nag me, Maby. I don't want to be like my father. I never have."

"I didn't say you had to be like your father. I just think you would be great at running a charity. You have a great personality for it, especially if you believed in it," Mabel argued.

But Mabel didn't know his father, so she had no idea what she was even talking about. She didn't know that his dad would never let him do something as meaningless as running part of the company. It was all or nothing. And "all" meant working side by side with the man for years, whereas "nothing" meant Cliff could be himself.

"Stop. I don't want to talk about it. And do not tell anyone. I don't want them to know." He leaned back in his chair.

"I'll keep your secret as long as you keep mine. I won't tell anyone that you are anything but the lazy bartender you pretend to be. Because that's all it is, you pretending to be something you are not."

"So judgy Mabel came back," he huffed.

"I'm not judging you, Cliff. I just don't understand. My family works for everything they get and works hard. You do nothing and walk away with an envelope of cash, just for being you." She leaned away from him, her arms now crossed, and her smile long gone.

"Is that what you think of me?" he demanded, hurt that she would think of him that way.

"Yes. I think you have a ton of potential that you're wasting by doing nothing."

"Well don't think about me then. Just go back to your perfect life and forget about me."

"I'm going to." She turned away from him and looked out the window.

Staring straight ahead of him, Cliff focused on his anger. He knew she was right, but she didn't have to rub it in his face. He loved his life and that he was in control of it. Nobody else had any say in any of it. Not even Mabel Lovely!

Neither of them spoke again as the plane landed, and they got off. Since both had only brought a carry-on, when he lost her in the airport crowd, he let her go. It was over; they were back in Minnesota. Now they were Mabel and Cliff and nothing else.

Suddenly all he wanted to do was find her in the crowd and drag her back to how it was when they were together. He was going to miss her, and she was going to be right there. Every time he turned around, she would be right there, and he would have to act like she was just Lucy's twin. For so long, he'd felt more connected to Lucy and only thought of Mabel as 'Lucy's twin.' But now, after spending the last four days with Mabel, he could only think of Lucy as Mabel's twin.

CHAPTER SEVENTEEN

RUBBING the remains of her tears from her face with the bottom of her T-shirt, Mabel climbed out of her Jeep in front of the house she was raised in. It was almost suppertime on a Thursday, so the house could be full or empty

Walking into the front door, she prayed nobody would be home. She needed time to think about the last couple of days with Cliff, to analyze it and get over any feelings she might have. But the couch was full of her sisters. All eyes turned away from the TV and looked right at her.

"Maby's home," Harper announced even though they could all see her.

"I'm home. What are we watching?" she asked as if she hadn't been gone for most of the week.

"Disney movie," Harper answered for the group, not even trying to disguise the loathing in her tone, but at least she stayed in the room.

"I will run this stuff upstairs and come back down," Mabel said, even as she planned to do the opposite.

At this point, Cliff was still foremost in her mind, and she hated how they had ended their time together. They were supposed to just walk away from each other after their vacation, not leave in anger. She had pissed him off for no reason. It was his life, after all. He could live it however he wanted to.

Up in her room, she had barely dumped her backpack and carry-on onto the bed before her door opened. Lucy rushed in, carrying two wine coolers in her hands. After setting them carefully on her dresser, Lucy gave Mabel a big hug. It was exactly what she needed. Any anger she had for her twin was completely gone in an instant.

"I missed you. Where have you been? Are you back? Don't leave like that again. I like to know where you are. Buzz has been sleeping in your bed." Lucy's words came out in a rush.

"Missed you too, you crazy woman. And I'll change the sheets." She looked at the bed in question.

"Where have you been?" Lucy let go of her finally and grabbed one of the bottles. She sat down on the bed and took a long drink.

"If I told you, then I wouldn't be able to go back when I need some alone time." No way was she telling her sister she'd been in Florida.

"I've been so lonely and bored without you. No one to talk to, no one to spend time with." Lucy flopped back on the bed but held her wine cooler upright, not even coming close to spilling it.

"You have five other sisters and Mom. And, as always, Cliff." Mabel reminded her, almost stumbling on his name.

"Cliff was gone to Florida. I was supposed to go with, but with everything happening the day we fought, I forgot to go," Lucy said, but it sounded off.

"Forgot? A vacation?" she asked, grabbing the beverage from her sister before she spilled it on the bed.

Lucy never forgot anything. Her amazing memory was what she was known for in the family. There was no way she would forget to go on a trip with her best friend.

"Okay, so maybe it was more like I didn't *want* to go. I mean, Kevin was going with his new girlfriend, so they would've been all over each other the entire time. And I hate going to new places."

"Since when?" Mabel took a drink of the wine cooler. It went down too easy.

"Since forever." Lucy took her drink back with a frown and pointed out the one on the dresser, the one she had brought for Mabel. "When Cliff started talking about the trip, we were both dating Kevin and Beth, but then they hooked up, and suddenly it felt weird. I mean, they're dating, and we're just friends. And we were going to share a room and a bed."

"But he sleeps over all the time. Are you saying you have never ...?" Mabel needed to know. She hated that she had slept with him if there was a possibility that he had slept with her twin. She didn't dare ask him at the time, fearing the answer. Still, she wondered if she was just a substitute for Lucy.

"No, never. I don't even think of him like that. I mean, he is good looking, but not my type." Lucy shrugged.

"Why not?"

"I don't know, I'm just not into him." Lucy's words frustrated Mabel. She wanted a real answer.

"Did you really go talk to Mr. Langley for me?" she asked, changing the subject. Though all she really wanted to do was talk about Cliff.

"Yes, and he's a stage-four creeper, Maby. I think you need to talk to someone about him. He tries to play all innocent, but he knows what he's doing," Lucy said, suddenly all serious.

"I have to talk to him on Monday. If I feel nervous, I'll go to the dean. If not, I will leave it." Though she always felt nervous and had never talked to the dean, not once.

"The guy across the hall said there was another lady who left a year before you came. I don't think it is just you. I may not be smart enough for college, but I know a lot about creeps," Lucy replied as her phone went off, but she ignored it.

"You're smarter than I am, Lucy." Mabel longed to bring up the dyslexia, but then she would have to say how she knew about it.

Lucy took another drink and rolled her eyes. "Right, college professor, you have always been the smart one."

"No, it just came easy for me. Maybe not so much for you," she said as Lucy's phone rang again. "Take it."

Lucy reluctantly took out her phone and answered without reading the name on the screen. "Lucy."

Mabel ignored her sister while she talked, opening her backpack and taking out her books and tablet, neither of which she had spent any time with. Cliff had taken up every moment they were together. Not that she regretted any of it.

"I'll ask her," Lucy said, bringing Mabel back. "Cliff wants us to go to the Grog for a while. I don't want to leave you since you just got here, but Cliff's been gone too."

Mabel smiled at her sister. She had known this would happen and would keep happening until he found someone new and didn't remember her anymore. She wished it was going to be that easy for her to forget him.

"No, I'm tired. You go, though. We have dress shopping in the morning."

"I'm in, but Maby's out," Lucy said into the phone as she got up off the bed and headed out the door. With a wave, she was gone.

Sitting on the vacated bed, Mabel gave herself a quick pep talk about not being jealous about her sister spending time with Cliff. After all, she had been invited, but Cliff knew she wouldn't go. And he knew why. But it wasn't the booze that made her stay home that night; it was that she wasn't strong enough to see Cliff. Not yet.

"How was sex with Cliff?" Agatha said from the doorway. She hadn't been downstairs when Mabel had come in the door. Mabel had thought she was out for the evening, but she must have been upstairs.

The house was warm, but Agatha was wearing a white sweatshirt and baggy orange shorts. She was never one for fashion, and it seemed she was in a "fuck it" mood today. But her hair was finally in a style that made her face look cute, or she had put on enough weight to fill out her face.

"No sex was had," she lied, as if Agatha would ever buy it.

"Right." Agatha chuckled and pointed at her. "Except that is the look of a sexed-up sister lusting for her sister's man."

"Nothing in that sentence is true, Ag," Mabel shot back.

"So, you two aren't a power couple now?" She leaned against the doorjamb.

"I think we are about the same. Cliff is Lucy's friend, and I am Lucy's sister," Mabel said. It was what they had agreed upon.

"Now if we could get Lucy out of that equation, you could ride away into the sunset together."

"When did your cynical heart turn romantic?" Mable shot back in surprise.

"When I see love, I push. Lord knows you people don't push yourselves. Look at Mom." She nodded at Sera's empty room down the hallway.

"You didn't do anything to help Mom," Mabel said.

"I would have if she didn't already know she loved him. Like you," Agatha argued as she grabbed Lucy's discarded wine cooler. She smelled it but didn't take a drink.

"I don't love him, and even if I did, he's a bartender with no ambition," Mabel said and tried half-heartedly to take the bottle from her sister. Only realizing belatedly that she was talking to her sister, who was a bartender, only because she hadn't been able to make a go of her art yet.

"So am I." Agatha's smile disappeared as she held the bottle away from her and walked out of the room with it.

Knowing she had hurt her sister didn't make Mabel feel any better than she had before, but she had no energy to apologize to Agatha at the moment. Not when she was hurting so much over her loss of Cliff.

CHAPTER EIGHTEEN

"LUCY!" Cliff called out to his best friend, instantly comparing her to her twin. They were identical but so different. And it was those differences that he liked better in one than the other. And suddenly, it was his friend who was lacking in the qualities he liked so much in Mabel.

When he had called Lucy, he had hoped that just seeing her would make him feel better about not seeing Mabel. But it hadn't worked. Seeing Lucy just made him miss Mabel twice as much, maybe even more. It just made him long for the real thing.

At first, Lucy said she wasn't going to come out because Mabel was home, but Mabel must have told her to go because she had decided to join him after all. For a second, he'd hoped that Mabel would come out too, but she had said no. He understood but felt she was missing out on so much by trying to constantly hide from alcohol. It was possible to go out and not drink, though he could see why she acted like she did.

"Cliff, you're back!" Lucy said as she made her way over and threw her arms around him. Holding her close, his body instantly recognized her as Lucy and was disappointed.

"I came back. How was it here?" He let her go, and she sat down across from him.

"Good. I was busy with Harper and work all week. Then with Mabel gone, I don't know. It was weird. I missed her even if I don't always talk to her. She's always been just across the hallway."

"You two have been apart before." Cliff ordered her a drink.

"Well, sure. I mean, she lived in the dorms for two years, and then she moved back. Maybe we needed to be apart then, but now I like to know where she is. Across the hallway. She is like my security blanket. I don't need it all the time, but I do like to know where it is." Lucy tapped her fingers against the table as she spoke.

"Well, she's back now. Hopefully she stays, so you don't have to be worried again." He wanted to keep talking about Mabel. He missed her so much even though they had only been apart a few hours. But he didn't want Lucy to know they had hooked up on vacation.

"How were Kevin and Beth?" Lucy looked around the bar, probably making sure that they hadn't shown up too. Lately, they seemed to show up at their favorite bar all the time.

"They looked good. I avoided them, mostly. I saw them at a bar one afternoon and another time outside their hotel room. We really didn't talk. Are you over him yet?" He hoped so because their conversation would surely get back to Lucy if she slept with him again.

"Yes, of course I am," she said unconvincingly.

"How about we get drunk and forget about everyone?" Cliff suggested. Namely her sister.

"Are you forgetting about Beth?" Lucy asked.

"Yeah," he lied because Beth was already forgotten. She had been much easier to get over than it was going to be to forget about Mabel.

Three hours later, he carried a very drunk Lucy into the Lovely house. The house was silent, but Lucy was not. She was singing and laughing despite his many attempts to shush her. Dropping her into her bed, he told her it was time to sleep, which she took as an excuse to sing louder, making him laugh. Lucy was always great fun when she was drunk.

Once she was in bed and despite her pleading that he stay, Cliff knew he wanted to go home. Lucy wasn't the Lovely he wanted to sleep with tonight, whether it was for sex or not. He didn't know if he could go back to just sleeping with Lucy.

Backing out of Lucy's room, he shut the door behind him. Turning, he looked at the door across the hallway. Mabel's room. He was ninety percent sure she was in there, sleeping. Lonely.

Since he had enough alcohol in his system to give him enough courage but not enough sense, he went across the hall and opened the door, just so he could see her. Worried someone might see him, he went inside the room and shut the door just in case.

Before he knew it, he was naked and slipping into bed with her, unable to stop himself. He needed her like his next breath in that moment.

As the bed sank under his weight, her brown eyes popped open. Her shock quickly turned to a grin as she moved closer to him and ran her hands up his chest and around his neck.

"Cliff," her voice was thick with sleep.

"Maby."

"We shouldn't," she whispered as her lips touched his chin.

"One more time," he whispered in response before his lips claimed hers, and he rolled her under him. He had missed just touching her these last few hours. And that was all it had been, hours. How was he going to last a day or more?

"Just. One. More. Time," she said as she kissed him over and over again.

It seemed that neither one was willing to give up tennis now that they were back home. Or maybe they just needed one more game.

CHAPTER NINETEEN

MABEL HADN'T BEEN able to fall to sleep after kicking Cliff out of her bed at 4 a.m. At the time, she had almost panicked that Harper would be up already because her sister sometimes had to start prepping for jobs at ungodly hours. But as far as she knew, Cliff was able to sneak out without anyone the wiser.

Of course, she knew she shouldn't have let him into her bed. They were done. But then he was there, and all she wanted was to be back in his arms for one more night. Though now she knew that one more night wasn't going to be enough; she wanted him there every night.

Sadly, hours later, in the cutest little dress shop in town, Cliff was on her mind, even as Mabel watched the happiest bride in the metro area cry giant tears. Agatha had just told her that in no way would she wear a bridesmaid dress. And on top of that, Agatha announced that she was not going to be one of Sera's seven bridesmaids either. Not only because it was a ridiculous amount, because she didn't want to be standing in front of everyone.

Agatha's decision was as predictable as Sera's tears. Maybe more so, because Sera knew what Agatha would say. It didn't matter whether the dress was pink or black; there was no way Agatha was going to wear it. Dressing up wasn't Agatha's thing and never had been. So far, she hadn't even tried a single dress on and had worn sweatpants and an oversized sweatshirt in black to prove her point. Even the sweatshirt said nothing on it, proving that Agatha wasn't into the day. She always wore a saying on her chest.

"Just say yes, Ag," Harper, as the oldest and bossiest sister, told her.

"No way. The woman can get married just as easy with me in a chair as me in a dress," Agatha argued. No way was she letting Harper push her around.

The standoff was on. It had been years since Harper had been able to actually tell Agatha what to do. Harper hated Agatha's unwillingness to do as she was told as much as Agatha hated Harper's tendency to boss her sisters around.

"Sera, do you want me to help you out of your dress so that you don't wreck it with tears before the wedding even happens?" Mabel got up and ushered her away from the scene because no amount of tears or anger were going to change the dark-haired woman's mind.

"I can get it myself, Maby," Sera protested as they went into the back of the store.

"No, you can't. You can't reach any of the buttons in the back," Mabel pointed out. It had taken two store attendants to get her into it fifteen minutes before. There had been no tears then, only "oohs" and "aahs" over how Sera had finally found *the* dress. Mabel couldn't control the tears when she saw her stepmom in the dress. Sera was gorgeous. Then, still in her dream wedding dress, Sera had turned her attention to finding dresses for her daughters.

"If I tried, I'm sure I could do it," Sera protested.

"Just let me help," Mabel said as they entered the oversized dressing room. There were nine white dresses hanging on hooks, but the one Sera was currently wearing was the right one. Everyone had agreed.

"What do you want?" her mom asked. Sera knew there was no other reason why Mabel would make her leave the battle. No one just walked away from a Lovely fight; that was admitting defeat.

"I just wanted to say that maybe Agatha doesn't want to wear a dress because of her weight gain. Have you thought of that?" Mabel spun her stepmom around and started on the bazillion buttons running down the back. Harrison was going to rip this thing off this woman after the wedding. He wasn't used to having this kind of patience.

"No, she looks better now. Get her in a dress, and she'll have to fight off the men," Sera said as she sucked in a breath. Maybe the dress was a little too small.

"We think that, but maybe Agatha is a little embarrassed by it still. You have to think about that when you're pushing her to be in the wedding. Her comfort before yours. Don't you ever remember being uncomfortable in your own skin? That's how Agatha is right now. Let her work that out on her own … not in front of strangers." Mabel tried not to point out that Sera's dream wedding dress wasn't going to be comfortable for hours on end. Or maybe it was just Mabel projecting because she didn't want to be in a wedding dress for hours on end.

"But I want her to be a part of it." Sera's voice cracked. The tears had come back.

"Have her design the programs or be your personal attendant. She'll enjoy that a lot more." Mabel finally got the last of the buttons undone and was glad she would never have to do that again.

Sera stopped holding up her dress and it fell to the floor, leaving her mostly naked. Dejected, she asked, "Do you want to be a bridesmaid?"

"No, but for you, I'd do anything. Even be a bridesmaid." Sera spun around and hugged Mabel.

"You're my favorite," she whispered into her hair.

"We both know Agatha is your favorite. Now treat her like it and don't make her wear a dress." She returned the hug.

"How are you after your time away from us? Feeling better?" Sera continued to hug her tight, which was a little awkward since she was just in her panties.

"In some ways, yes, in others, no. Life is a rocky road." She pushed her mom away and picked up the white dress as Sera stepped around it.

"They need to have that on ice cream cartons. Have you told Lucy?" Sera pulled on a Grand Cannon shirt, finally covering her naked breasts. Mabel had long gotten over how comfortable most of her family was being naked, even in public. Even her.

"What?" She almost dropped the dress at the words. There was so much in her life that Lucy didn't know suddenly.

"About Cliff sneaking out of your room this morning." Sera grinned as she pulled on her jeans. Little got past that woman, even with her busy life, fiancé, and a wedding in two months.

"That did not happen," Mabel said in denial.

"Not what I saw. Violet had a nightmare, and I was bringing her back to her room. Then what did I see?" Sera was still grinning at her.

"It's nothing. It's over. We aren't compatible," Mabel replied.

"More compatible than him and Lucy," said Sera, emphasizing the word compatible.

"They aren't like that," Mabel protested. Every time she had asked Lucy or Cliff, they swore their relationship was purely platonic.

"Have you talked to them both? That should be your first step, now that you and Lucy are talking again. Talk to her. You might be surprised about her feelings for him. And his for her. You need everything on the table before you go any further. Then you can explore your feelings for each other. But you can't hide this from Lucy; you both love her too much." Mabel knew her stepmom would be watching. Sera was an overprotective mom with anyone who might hurt her kids.

"It was just a few days of a fling, and it's over now. We're both going back to our lives."

"Yesterday or today? Or tomorrow? Next week?" Sera answered, jumping up from the bench. "Should we start looking for a white dress for you too?"

"What?" Mabel looked around the room of wedding dresses, her mind immediately going to Cliff ripping a tight, bazillion-button dress off her body because he couldn't control himself.

"A dress. You could be next Mrs. Clifford Scott." Sera chuckled.

"Clifton, and no. No way in hell." She didn't want to look at the dresses anymore, so she walked out of the room, leaving her mom laughing at her.

The battle was still going strong when she got out into the main part of the shop. Harper and Buzz were trying to bribe Agatha into being a bridesmaid. They were up to laundry and baked goods for a year. Maybe some cash, Lucy was pushing the cash angle, as if she had any to spare.

Behind her, Sera announced, "Leave Agatha alone, she doesn't feel comfortable in a dress. So, she can create the announcements and programs, and she'll be my personal slave for the day."

"Attendant." Mabel shook her head.

"That." Sera pointed at Mabel.

The look of relief that crossed Agatha's face made Mabel want to hug her. It looked like she had been holding her own with the negotiations, but they seemed to have bothered her more than she had let on.

Smiling at her, Mabel shrugged, hoping she would be forgiven for accusing her of just being a bartender. Everyone knew that Agatha was only a bartender because her art hadn't taken off yet. One day it would, and everything would be alright for the woman. Until that day, the entire family would have her back.

"Since we have everyone here—including our wayward Maby—let's go out to lunch. Who wants what?" Sera announced, and everyone had an opinion, everyone but Mabel and Agatha. Both were usually the passive ones when it came to meals. Harper was a food snob, so she usually got her way with restaurants.

"Thanks, Maby," Agatha whispered as the group began to argue over Italian versus Japanese.

"If you don't want to be a bridesmaid, you shouldn't have to. I just explained that your talents could be used in other ways," Mabel said quietly.

"You just want to be off the hook about having sex last night." Agatha winked at her and turned back to the discussion. It seemed Agatha's gratitude only went so far before it was over.

Mabel knew her face was red with embarrassment. Now two of her family knew. Or one knew for sure, and one thought they knew. Cliff's name wasn't said, but it didn't have to be.

Somehow, she had made it an entire day in Florida with Cliff not knowing who she was but hadn't lasted twelve hours without her family finding out about her and Cliff.

CHAPTER TWENTY

Saturday night found Cliff working his usual gig at the Grog. There was a band playing, and the place was packed, but Cliff couldn't really feel it tonight. Tonight, the fun of mixing drinks and watching people was lost on him. He was bored.

Since he had left Mabel's bed, he'd done nothing but think about her and come up with ways to keep her. Or get her back. Whichever one it was. But nothing short of actually getting a job and being an adult would do the trick. And at this point, he wasn't ready for that, if he was ever going to be ready for that.

"Cliff, do you have those guys handled?" Nick asked him, getting a bit angry at his lack of concentration.

"Yeah, I got them," he replied as he went over to the college kids who were gathered at the end of the bar, waiting.

Smiling at them, he wished he had not come in that night. No way was he in the mood for college kids. As they ordered, Cliff filled their drinks as fast as he could, but with so many of them, he had a hard time. Though he had done this hundreds of times, he wasn't in the zone today, and it showed.

"Hey buddy, can you bring our drinks sometime today?" a blond guy asked sarcastically, making his friends laugh.

Letting the words roll of his back, Cliff took the money from a blue-eyed chick who winked at him as he handed over a shot of tequila. Whatever the wink meant, he didn't care. Right now, there was only one woman he wanted to sleep with, and it wasn't this young thing.

Almost every night he worked, some woman would hit on him. He was used to it, and most of the time, he enjoyed the attention. A week ago, he would have flirted back, maybe to the point of taking her home. But tonight, he wasn't interested.

"What are you doing, Jolie? Are you hitting on the bartender?" a tall, athletic blond guy asked behind her, his voice mocking.

"Never mind, Tyson," the blue-eyed woman told her friend and drank down the shot. Then asked for another one.

"Guys, guys," Tyson pretended to whisper to his buddies. "Jolie's hitting on the old guy behind the bar.

"Sorry," she mouthed, taking the second shot from him before turning back to her friends.

Shaking his head, Cliff hoped the night would speed by. His entire carefree life had gotten old in a short time. He wondered what Mabel was doing. He knew this afternoon, she was going with her sisters to go dress shopping for Sera, but after that, he had no idea. Maybe her sisters talked her into going out on the town, or maybe she was at home watching movies with the littlest two so that everyone else could go out. Or, more likely, so she could hide her past from them.

In the back corner of the bar, he watched Jolie take a few drinks from her friend's glasses, and at one point, she swallowed a pill, downing it with a vodka tonic from Tyson. The girl was wasted, and when rounds were bought for the group, he didn't add her drink choice. But she kept drinking anyway; everyone willing to share.

Turning his eyes to the rest of the bar, he ignored the group until a commotion in the corner brought him back from his thoughts of Mabel. The crowd parted, and Cliff jumped out from behind the bar to stop the fight. But when he got there, he realized it wasn't a fight—the blue-eyed girl had passed out on the floor.

"Call an ambulance!" he yelled into the crowd.

"She just passed out, man. She's been drinking a lot." The blond guy was crouched down near her but didn't seem too concerned about her. Nor were any of those who had been giving her drink after drink.

Ignoring the guy, he checked for a pulse but found none. Instantly, he started CPR, something he had never done on a human before. A lady broke from the crowd and started helping him. She seemed more experienced, and he was thankful for her help, but the girl still didn't wake up or breathe on her own.

Watching the woman as she worked over Jolie and finally got her to breathe on her own, Cliff was scared to death for her. For her and her family, for anyone's life she had touched and would miss her if she didn't make it. And for Mabel, who went through this same thing.

Within minutes the paramedics were there and pushing him and the lady to the side. By the time they took her away, most of the crowd in the bar was gone, the near-death killing their buzz. Cliff wasn't too sure she would make it.

"What happened to her?" the lady who had helped asked from beside him.

"I don't know. She must have drunk too much. She was already drunk when she came into the bar. I stopped serving her, but I think her friends kept giving her more. And I saw her take something." His eyes went to Tyson, who was sitting at a table, his back to them as he ignored the entire thing, as were his buddies.

Images of Mabel replaced the ones of the blue-eyed girl. Mabel's friends hadn't cared enough about her to stop her. They hadn't even been there to see her or help her. Before he knew what he was doing, he was on the kid, pounding his fists into the guy's face. He knew it wasn't for Jolie, but for Mabel.

Cliff got in more than a few punches before Nick dragged him away. The kid's nose was bleeding and so was his lip.

"What the hell, man?!" the kid asked, wiping the blood away.

"What did you give her?" Cliff demanded, even though he had no proof. His mind was back on Mabel and not in the present. The anger was for her, even if he knew it wasn't this guy's fault.

"Nothing. She always takes pills when she drinks. What's it to you?"

"She could have died tonight! She still might! Don't you care?"

"Why do you care?" the guy was holding his nose as he asked, acting completely innocent.

"Because someone has to." He shook himself free of Nick's grasp, his anger dissipating because that girl wasn't Mabel. Mabel was okay. She was with her family and okay.

Without a word, he walked out the door. He was done for tonight. Hopefully, he would feel better in a few days when he had to work again because tonight, being a bartender sucked.

Walking into his apartment a few minutes later, he could hear Brad and his girlfriend in the back bedroom. Rolling his eyes, he flopped onto the couch only to sit on a slice of pizza that was left there. Tossing it on the coffee table, he turned on the TV but was met with nothing but snow on the screen. After spending a few minutes with no luck trying to find a station that actually worked, he shut it off again.

With nothing better to do, he headed back out, away from his mess of a life. Was it this bad before he left for Florida, or was it only bad now because Mabel said it was? Was she right about him not even trying to be an adult? Should he consider being an adult?

Should he get a job that paid better, something that made a difference? Perhaps move into his own place and not survive on take out? Go out with his friends less, drink less. Change completely?

His mindless walking led him to one place, the place he felt most at home: the Lovely house. Walking inside without knocking, he found a few of the sisters watching TV. All eyes turned to him before turning back to the screen. His presence wasn't anything new.

The one woman he wanted to see wasn't there. Hiding his disappointment, he kicked off his shoes and sat down next to Lucy, hoping that just being in the same house as Mabel would be enough.

"I thought you were working." Lucy handed him a beer from the coffee table. It was not very cold anymore, but that didn't matter.

"It had gotten quiet, so I left," he lied, not wanting to get into the truth.

"We're doing a movie marathon, *Star Wars* in the order they were released. No prequel stuff tonight," Lucy informed him.

"Sounds fun." He could get into the marathon idea. He needed to take his mind off how his life wasn't as great as he thought it was.

"It has been. We started at 4 p.m."

"Where's everyone else?" he asked, wanting to know where Mabel was but knowing he couldn't just ask about her.

"Sera and Harrison are on a date, as if he still needs to date her. He has her tied down. Harper is on a date with Grant—he for sure doesn't have that one locked down. Agatha and Violet are upstairs," Lucy finished.

With Lucy and Buzz watching movies with Emma, that left only one sister. But Lucy didn't mention where Mabel was. Sadly, she was that only one he truly wanted to see or hear about.

Two hours later, the TV finally got shut off as the siblings headed to bed, Buzz giggling as she headed to Sera's room so she would have a bed for the night. Without thinking, he followed Lucy like he always did.

Turning into her room, he looked at Mabel's closed door, wishing he had the balls to go into her room instead. Except tonight he had no idea if she was even in there. No word had been said about her all evening, and he hadn't dared ask.

He should just tell Lucy what happened. He didn't know if she would be mad. If she remembered the night they had sex, then she would be pissed. Or maybe she would be pissed anyway, knowing that he wasn't good enough for Mabel in the first place.

CHAPTER TWENTY-ONE

It was Harper's mixer that woke Mabel from sleep. She had gone to sleep the night before around seven o'clock. Apparently, Florida had taken a lot out of her, and nobody had warned her that dress shopping was so exhausting. That should have been discussed before she had agreed to it.

Getting up, she was happy the bathroom wasn't full so she could shower before going down to see who all was up. Once done, she put on jeans and a T-shirt, this one was purple and said "Hort" on it. So far, nobody had come up with what it should have said.

Knowing that she was fixing her hair because she wanted to be prepared in case Cliff wandered over made her mad, but it didn't stop her from doing it. Mabel grumbled even as she tried to make herself look a little better than normal for him. In a little way, she wanted to show him that she was worth something.

When she finally made it into the kitchen, Harper and Buzz were the only ones there. Buzz was still in her pajamas, explaining an article she was supposed to write for the paper. Harper was barely paying attention, her full concentration on the bread she was kneading.

"Morning," Mabel called as she walked in.

"Wow, showered already. Making the rest of us look bad," Harper said without stopping her kneading. Her body was covered in a chef's jacket, which meant she hadn't changed before coming down. Buzz, as usual, was in a blue T-shirt that said Buzzzz on it and shorts, all of which she had slept in. Her special-made shirts with her name on them were always her favorite pajamas.

"The bathroom was empty. I think I'll get up at four every morning so I can get some bathroom time." She sat down on the stool next to Buzz.

"Sometimes it's full, so don't set your alarm just for that." Harper tossed her dough into a bowl. Due to her work hours, which were 4 a.m. to noon, she was telling the truth.

"Thank god. I can't get up this early every day," Mabel said with a laugh, hoping her sisters had stopped talking about her. "What are you doing up so early, Buzz?"

"Mom came home. I didn't think she would be back this early. I was hoping to sleep in today."

"I'm done with my bed if you want it," Mabel offered.

Buzz looked at her for a second, as if analyzing her. "I'll do that. I need my beauty rest, and Harps isn't listening to me anyway."

"Go ahead, but don't think I'm just going to let you keep it. I don't want to be on the couch," Mabel said as Buzz left the room.

The kitchen went silent as Harper covered her bread dough with a towel and started to work on getting breakfast ready. Though their usual day to gather was Saturday, it had been cut short by the dress shopping. Harper slid a pan of leftover chicken into the oven, and Mabel knew her other sisters would be showing up very soon.

"What are those from?" Mabel asked, pointing to the chicken.

"Corporate lunch on Wednesday. They requested we bring enough for thirty, and only ten showed up. But we still charged them for thirty." Harper waved her hand over the large pan of extra chicken. Most of it was still in the plastic container because there was only so much the family eat in the morning. Leftovers were typically 'thrown out' by the chef in catering businesses. Needless to say, the Lovely food bill was usually quite small.

"Can I ask you something, and can you keep it between us?" Mabel wanted to keep Lucy's secret to herself but knew she needed to talk to someone. Harper spent the most time with Lucy, had for a few years. They were closer than she was with Lucy these days.

Harper put the plastic container back in the fridge. Turning back to Mabel, she had a grin on her face and leaned against the counter. Harper loved gossip. "Sure, I don't talk to anyone."

"Does Lucy ever do the paperwork for your company?"

"What do you mean?" Harper straightened up, instantly offended by the question.

"Like put things in the computer or fill out forms? Things like that." Mabel pushed on.

"Some. I guess I'm too much of a control freak to let her. That side has been my job since I began the business. I mean, at first, she just worked for me on jobs, then moved into sort of a partner when she was there all the time anyway. Why? Did she complain? Does she think I should let her do everything? Then what would I do?" Harper demanded, her back up at the question.

"No, not at all. Just something I've been turning over in my head." Mabel wished she hadn't asked. She had already known the answer, based on both of her sister's personalities.

"Is she saying that I don't let her do enough? I just want to make sure it is done right, and Lucy is ..." Harper stopped talking and turned away from her to dig in the fridge.

"Not smart?" Mabel filled in the blank.

"I didn't say that. You did." Harper slammed a jug of orange juice on the counter.

"Then why don't you let her be in charge more? You're always the lead on your jobs. You're in control. Why not let her take over sometime?" Mabel pushed.

"Hello, Maby, I'm a control freak. This has been established over the years. I just run with it now." She picked up the juice again only to slam it down once more.

"I know, Harper. I *am* the next oldest." Mabel put up her hands in case the juice was about to come her way next.

Harper stopped and glared at her. "What is this all about? Do you want me to give Lucy more responsibility? I don't know if she even wants that. I see and talk to her every day. I think I know her a little better than you do, Maby. Even if you are twins."

"Nothing. Forget I said anything," Mabel replied, wishing someone else would come down. Anyone else.

"No, no I won't. What is this about?" Harper pressed, her tone lighter as she walked around the island, the juice forgotten.

"Just something I've been thinking about." She shrugged as she watched Harper sit down next to her in the seat Buzz had been sitting in. Possibly too close.

"What?" Harper bumped her shoulder with hers.

"Nothing." Mabel didn't bump back. Harper put her arm around her shoulders.

"Something." Harper put her other arm around her and hugged her.

"Harper?" Mabel questioned as Harper's hug got tighter and tighter until she couldn't move anymore.

"Tell Harper, Maby, and you will not get hurt," Harper finally threatened.

"I'm already hurt," she admitted. Harper had been making too much dough lately—her arms were strong.

"Talk, Mabel Lucie!" Harper demanded again, dropping the nice act now that she had her sister trapped.

Wiggling to get free, Mabel only managed to get Harper's arms tighter around her. "Let go, Harper."

"Not until you tell me the truth."

"No." She jerked her body, only to push them off the stools, sending both to the floor in a thump. Harper managed to stay holding on to her throughout the fall. Unfortunately, now she was lying on top of Mabel and had her completely in her control. Maby couldn't move at all.

"Tell me." Harper let go of Mabel as she was sitting on her hand and used her other to push Mabel's head into the floor. One of her fingers was digging into her eye.

"Harper, let her go," Sera demanded from the doorway.

"Nope, she's lying to me." Harper's grip didn't let up. In fact, she tightened it until Mabel thought that her eye might be damaged.

"Don't lie to your sister, Maby," Sera scolded even as she pushed Harper off.

"This isn't over," Harper insisted as she sat on the floor glaring at her.

"I think I'm done for today." Mabel felt around her eyes, face, and back of her head for damage as she left the kitchen. At this point, she wasn't ready to tell Lucy's secret, if she was ever going to be. It wasn't her place to tell anyone else, it was Lucy's.

CHAPTER TWENTY-TWO

LEAVING the Lovely house early Sunday morning should have been a breeze. Lucy had woken early for someone who'd been up late and had a hangover. Once she jumped in the shower, Cliff decided it was time to head out, thus avoiding as many of the Lovely women as possible.

Grabbing his phone from the dresser, he headed out of Lucy's room and came face to face with Mabel's door. The room he wanted to be in, the room he wished he was sneaking out of this morning. Or not sneaking, just leaving like he was leaving Lucy's. He was tired of sneaking.

Sliding his phone in his pocket, he cursed himself for his weakness as he listened to the house around him. Voices filtered up from downstairs, and he could hear the shower was running, but no other sound was coming from the second or third floors of the house.

He quietly opened her door across the hall, just to catch a peek of her sleeping form. It had been only a day, but to Cliff, it seemed like a lifetime had passed since he had seen her or touched her. He wanted to just see her.

Swinging the door open enough to stick his head in, he looked at her tucked beneath her purple comforter. Her hair spread out across the pillow as she slept—her red hair.

Buzz sat up and looked at him in confusion as he backed out and shut the door. Why was Buzz in Mabel's bed? Buzz only got a bed if a sister was going to be out of the house all night. Who had Maby been with all night that Buzz got to sleep in her bed?

And Buzz had seen him. Maybe he could play off being drunk still if she asked about it. It was an easy lie since they had been drinking together the night before—the night Mabel had been unaccounted for.

Cursing under his breath, he headed down the stairs, hoping Buzz wouldn't tell everyone, but he was pretty sure she would. Halfway down the stairs, he saw Sera walking into the living room with a bag of peas in her hand.

"Here, put this on your eye. It'll get the swelling down." Sera handed the peas to the person resting on the couch with their bare feet on the arm rest.

"Tell Harper she's a shithead," came Mabel's voice from the couch.

The relief that washed through Cliff at the sound of her voice made him trip on the last step, causing everyone to look his way. But it didn't matter, Mabel was there, not in some guy's bed all night. Some guy who wasn't him.

"Careful, Cliff," Sera said as she arranged the peas on Mabel's face. "We don't have any more peas. You would have to settle for beans or a box of ice cream."

"I'm okay, Mom Lovely," he said, his eyes on Mabel and not on Sera at all. The bag of peas was pressed to her right eye. He wanted to ask her what happened and make sure she was okay, except they weren't a couple, and he didn't want to draw anymore suspicion than he already had today.

"Good, one injury a day in this house is enough," Sera said as she looked at him—scrutinized him, more like it. After knowing her for a year, he could tell when she was analyzing him, though he never knew exactly why she ever did it.

"Well, I'd better head home," he announced, heading for the door.

"As if you have a home, Cliff. You basically live here," Sera mumbled as she got to her feet and headed back to the kitchen. She must have decided Mabel would survive.

Stopping near the door, he could stop himself from asking, "You okay, Maby?"

"Yeah, Harper got a little rough this morning." She didn't smile; she just stared at him. Was it because she knew he had slept with her sister? Did it seem as wrong to her as it felt to him?

"Be safe," he said and left the house, wishing he could kiss the bruise her sister had caused, followed by the lips that he longed to taste. Then he wanted to spend the day protecting her from her sisters and the damage that they inflicted in name of love.

Back at his apartment, he found it was still a mess. Brad hadn't cleaned anything; he had only made it more of a disaster. Leaving it as it was, he changed into his running clothes and took a long run through the city. He missed the beach and ocean views. He missed returning to Mabel when he was done.

Without paying attention to where he was going, his mind drifted to Mabel and her words. Was he wasting his life? He had never thought he had been wasting it; he had always just wanted to live it and not be what and who his dad was.

Clifton Scott IV had barely been there when he was growing up, leaving most of the child-rearing to his mother. Even after their divorce when Cliff was seven, nothing changed; months would go by without him seeing his father. But the moment Cliff wasn't living up to the Scott name, Daddy was there. His dad paid for Prep school and even an Ivy League college; nothing but the best for a Scott. No matter what he tried out for, he made the team or got the part. All it took was enough money, which meant it didn't take him long to stop trying because everything would be handed to him anyway. At twenty-four, he still had no degree and didn't even want the ones he could get. He had dropped out of college and had started living life like he wanted to. He wished for a life where he didn't need money, so he didn't even try to make it. And never once did he throw around money to make friends; he hadn't needed to.

That had been years ago, and he was still just doing that: living for himself. He had always though he was like wild and crazy Lucy, except

Lucy had goals and dreams, which he lacked. Every day, she worked to make her dreams come true. He did nothing.

Back in the apartment, Brad's bedroom door was open, and the apartment seemed empty. After a quick shower, he started to clean the place up. After filling four garbage bags with just food containers, he knew he didn't want to live like this. He needed a new place, a place that wasn't a mess … a place without Brad in it.

Suddenly, he wanted a place to be proud of and bring women to, or just one. As of now, the one he wanted wouldn't step foot in this place. No matter what happened or didn't happen in the Lovely house, it was always clean. The girls could be sloppy pigs at times, but they mostly cleaned up after themselves. It had been one of the first things Lucy had taught him: how to clean up after himself. Because she wasn't going to do it for him.

Getting a better place would call for more money, and his bartending would never provide enough for that. Maybe Mabel was right, and he should try and work for his dad. As long as he could remember, the only job available for him at Scott International was president, but Mabel had shown him that there were many other jobs that he could possibly do.

Pulling out his phone, he searched his contacts for his dad's number, listed as POS. His dad answered with his usual confidence and constant annoyance. "Clifton, you are alive."

"Yes, Dad, I am. Thanks for caring." The old man could have called him just as easily as Cliff had today. That never happened.

"I care. I hear you saw your grandma recently." There was a creak of leather as his dad adjusted in his chair.

"Yup." He wondered where his dad had heard that.

"Getting married, are you? And now you need a job? Because bartending doesn't pay for a wife." The voice held nothing but condescension.

"Where did you hear I was getting married?" he demanded, not caring about the job anymore. Who was his source?

"Babs told your mom, and she told me. You had better call her soon. She's having a hard time not getting excited for the wedding, but she can't get excited if you haven't told her," his dad said.

"When do you talk to Mom?" Cliff sat down on the couch, unable to hide his surprise. He hadn't thought the couple had talked in years. His parents had had a bitter divorce over twenty years ago. They had fought all his life.

Now it sounded like they had turned into friends? When had that happened, and why had he never known about it?

"Often. Just because we aren't married doesn't mean we have nothing to talk about. Like you."

"But you two didn't get along, ever."

"We did. Just not as a married couple. As a divorced couple, we're great. Not getting remarried great, but friends. So, who is this special lady?"

"Her name is Mabel, and we aren't really getting married," he admitted.

"Not yet, son. But now you have time to get a job and settle into being an adult. Then you can afford a wife and a home she deserves. Once you start working here, you can. You can start tomorrow as my right-hand man and learn the job that you'll be doing when I step down. Learn to be just like me." His dad had just mapped out the life that had Cliff never wanted and still didn't want. Not even for Mabel. He would rather be broke with Mabel than have her see him turn into his father.

"What? I don't want to be you. In fact, I have never wanted to be you, and I will never want to be you." Cliff couldn't hide the scorn in his voice, nor did he try. His father would never let him be less than head of the company, a position he wasn't ready for and didn't even want.

"Cliff." His dad's voice was stern.

"Forget I called. I don't need anything from you." He hung up on his father, as he usually did.

Grabbing his keys, Cliff headed out of the house to see his mom, who was apparently his dad's friend now, to inform her he was not getting married and probably never would be.

CHAPTER TWENTY-THREE

MONDAY MORNING, Mabel was finally feeling ready to get back to her life again. The rumors should have dissipated or hopefully gone away completely. She needed to get her lesson plans done and to Kirk for approval by Friday. Taking last week off had been a mistake. A much-needed mistake, but still a mistake. Now she had only a week to get her lessons complete and approved.

While opening a book and marking the passages she wanted to reference, she nearly jumped out of her seat when Kirk said from the doorway, "Miss Lovely."

The way he said her name grated on her ears. Over the years, she hadn't noticed it could double as an endearment until some sleazy guy had pointed it out. It was always the sleazy ones.

"Hi, Kirk. I'm almost done with my lesson plan," she said, waving the book at him.

"I'm sure it's going to be great. Everything you do is." Kirk took a step inside the room, making the tight space even tighter. Why was it only when he came in that her office felt small? When she had four freshmen in here last fall, it had been fine. Kirk wasn't even that big of a guy.

"You'll just have to check it to find out, but it's not ready yet. I think by this afternoon, it'll be ready enough to send to you." Mabel tried to hold her ground even though she remained sitting in her chair.

He sneered at her. "I like your twin. You never said you had one. And her name is Lucy, even."

"I guess we don't usually run in the same circles, so I don't bring her up." And since this was her job, she shouldn't have to bring up the fact that she had a twin.

"You should have her visit more often. She's very nice to look at." His words made her wonder if it was his way of complimenting her since they were identical. Though they liked to pretend otherwise, they were. So far, at nearly thirty, they still looked very similar.

"She's busy at her job, so we usually don't see each other much." Spinning back to her computer, she tried to give him the hint that she was busy—too busy to talk about her sister, the one she saw all the time.

"Then I'll just have to settle for you." His hands rested lightly on her shoulders. "But I won't be settling."

Flying from her chair and away from him, Mabel went to the furthest corner from him, which could have been any of them since he was in the middle of the room and not five feet from away her still. Crossing her arms over her chest as her heart beat rapidly, Mabel tried to figure out how to get out of this. Kirk's awkward advances were the opposite of subtle that day.

"Kirk, I told you there is nothing between us. That it was all a misunderstanding."

"But that was before you took a week off and didn't inform anyone, Mabel Lucie." Kirk smiled innocently at her.

"I did tell someone. I emailed you about it," she replied, wishing she had told someone else, but he was the person she was supposed to get approval from. Now she was seeing how she had walked right into a trap.

"I could go through my emails again." He reached for his phone, then stopped. "After we go out tonight." He acted like he had just thought it up.

Looking at the weasel, she wondered what Lucy would do in this scenario. Lucy always knew how to handle a situation. Lucy would be able to outsmart him, but Mabel was stuck, unable to even think.

"Where and when?" she hissed through her teeth. He had her; her career was in his hands, and he knew it. There was no way she could go to the dean now. It was his word against hers, and he was head of the department. An email wasn't how she should have asked for time off; she should have called. But his behavior had made that impossible.

A smile crept over his face as he named a restaurant downtown she had heard of but had never been to. Now she had mere hours to come up with a plan to save her career but not let the weasel try anything with her.

With only an hour to go before she had to meet Kirk, Mabel was still pacing in her bedroom. No plan had come to her. At least, nothing that wouldn't send her career into the toilet. Stepping out of her room in despair, she ran right into Agatha in the hallway.

Mabel looked ready in a blue dress and heels—ready to end her career, because she was not doing anything with that weasel. *Ever*.

"Sorry, Ag, didn't see you there," she mumbled.

"Look at you all dressed up and nervous." Agatha chuckled. "Hot date with a mystery man? Are you nervous about his buddy finding out?"

"No, just my boss." She turned to leave, not wanted to get into it. The one silver lining about Kirk's proposal was that she hadn't thought about Cliff in hours.

"Wait, wait, wait. Your sleazy boss? Why?" Agatha grabbed Mabel's arm, stopping her in the middle of the hallway. Her face was no longer happy but a bit pissed off, which was emphasized by the fact that she was wearing a red hooded sweatshirt with the hood up. She looked like a thug, a short thug in long shorts and with bare feet.

"What's going on out here?" Lucy came out of her room. As far as Mabel could see, it was empty. No Cliff. She cursed herself for looking all the time!

"Maby's going on a date with her sleazy boss," Agatha informed her sister.

"Why? You can't date him. He's gross! Did you report him?" Lucy asked.

"No, he hadn't done anything that bad," Mabel informed them. At least not until he blackmailed her into a date, and now it was too late to do anything about it.

"Then why are you going out with him?" Agatha asked.

"Because he said I didn't ask for last week off, so I can be fired. I only emailed him." Mabel's shoulders slumped as she admitted her failure. She hated being a failure.

"Your email is in your sent items on your computer, Maby. You just have to show the dean and tell him what Sleezo's doing." Lucy acted like she knew something about computers. As far as Mabel knew, she didn't even have one.

"Whether I sent it or not doesn't matter. He didn't open it. He demanded a date and then said he'd look for the email. Until then, my career in his hands," Mabel stated. All her hard work was going to be for nothing.

"Are you going to fuck him? Because that's what he wants." Agatha leaned against the wall, and Mabel saw her face clearly for the first time today. She looked tired with dark bags under her eyes. She looked how Mabel felt.

"I'm not sleeping with him. Ever. But right now, he has my career in his hands, and I don't want to lose that. I've worked too hard to lose that," Mabel admitted.

"I have an idea. Agatha, take Mabel's computer and find the email and take screenshots of it. I'll call Cliff." Lucy was rubbing her hands together.

"Cliff?" Mabel asked, thankful to be able to say his name out loud again. Even just this once.

"Yes, Cliff. I'm going to have him meet you at the restaurant after you've been there a few minutes. Take your phone and record everything until he gets there. The weasel thinks he has you, but he's in for a rude awakening. Don't fuck with a Lovely!"

Lucy pulled out her phone and went into Mabel's room where Agatha was already sitting on the bed with her computer on her lap.

"I don't know if this will work." Her voice was cracking because she loved her sisters so much. They would do anything for her. Both of them. And what did she do in return? Hurt Agatha's feelings, and sleep with Lucy's best friend. She was scum.

"My plans always work. Do you remember what Cliff looks like?" Lucy asked as she held her phone to her ear, waiting for Cliff to answer.

"Yes," Mabel said as Agatha smirked at her from the bed. Lucy didn't notice.

"Go, then. He'll be there as quickly I can get him there," she said to Mabel, then to the phone, "Cliff, we have an emergency."

Mabel walked out the door feeling better. She drove to the restaurant, and as she parked, she got a message from Lucy alerting her that Cliff was on his way. It wasn't how she wanted to see him, but she would be grateful when he showed up.

Kirk was already seated when she went inside the restaurant, his smarmy smile already in place. Mabel placed her phone on the table as she sat right where he could see it, and it could pick up his voice the best. He was dressed in the same clothes he had on earlier in the day. The only difference was that they were now wrinkled.

"You came, Mabel Lucie. I didn't think you would," he admitted.

"It was either this or end my career, right?" Mabel didn't hide the fact that she didn't want to be here.

"Now, that isn't how I see it, Mabel Lucie. I just thought we could get something to eat and get to know each other better," he answered, sidestepping his ultimatum.

"I think we know each other fairly well," she stated and took a drink of the waiting water.

"But it's a more relaxed atmosphere here." He looked around the room, which was busy and not the most intimate restaurant in the area.

"So, you're going to admit you received the email I sent you?" she asked, hoping to get this over with before anything actually happened.

"What email? I get many throughout the day." He smirked and picked up his menu.

"The email informing you that I was taking five days off," she reminded him, not picking up hers.

"I just don't remember that email. But I remember us dancing, do you?" he asked over his menu.

"No, because it wasn't me." Which he knew, now that he had met Lucy.

"I know it was your twin, but it should have been you because we would be perfect together. You and me, me and you." He set his menu down and leaned toward her.

His moving just that much closer to her made her push her chair away from the table a little more. He had always given her bad vibes, but they had just gotten worse over the last few hours. Even looking at him disgusted her now.

"There is no you and me," Mabel reminded him.

"Not yet, but it'll happen. We're on the first steps of the journey."

"No, we are not." Mabel's heart soared as she saw Cliff walk into the restaurant. He was wearing a suit and tie and looked like the billionaire he was. The grey material clung to his body in just the right places. He looked as good in a suit as he did in shorts and a T-shirt. "I have a boyfriend."

"No, you don't. You would have said something sooner." Kirk's smile dropped suddenly.

"We went on vacation together."

"You were staying with friends." As if she ever told him that.

"Just one, a man." She held up her finger and pointed at the man in question.

"Hey, beautiful. Sorry I'm late. My meeting went long," Cliff said and bent down and kissed her on the lips, not a peck, but deep enough to not be proper for a public ... kiss.

"Cliff." She sighed when his lips finally left hers, easily forgetting they were in the middle of a restaurant in front of her boss.

"Mabel Lucie?" Kirk demanded.

"Sorry." She reluctantly turned away from Cliff but didn't remove herself from his arms as she introduced the two. It had been too long since she'd felt his touch. "Kirk, this is my boyfriend, Cliff Scott."

Cliff smiled as he reached out and shook the other man's hand. "Well, Mabel Lucie misspoke. I'm her fiancé. She agreed to marry me on the plane ride to Florida just last week. It's so new, she forgets sometimes."

"Mabel Lucie has told me nothing about you," Kirk pouted.

Cliff basically ignored the man as he helped Mabel back into her seat and then sat down in the formerly empty chair between her and Kirk. Once settled, he turned his full attention on the other man.

"She's told me a lot about you, Langley." Cliff was no longer the happy, jovial guy he always was. He was pissed.

"I assure you, there is nothing going on with us," Kirk defended himself.

"If I hear of one more time that you made my fiancé feel uncomfortable, ever, I will end your career." Cliff's words were clipped.

Mabel nearly swooned at the way he took command and threatened the man. She wasn't typically one for alpha men, but right now, Mabel could get on board with Alpha Cliff. It was turning her on, and not just a little. She hoped one day Alpha Cliff would show up in her bed.

"You have no control over me," Kirk shot back with a smirk.

"I do believe the new administration building, where your dean works, and your checks are cut, is called the Clifton Scott Administration Building. My grandfather gave the money for that to be built. I'm sure that even you know the dean will do whatever I tell him to." His hand wrapped around her leg under the table possessively.

"Are you threatening me?"

"It's only a threat if you make Mabel Lucie's life uncomfortable again. But if I were you, I would consider finding another university to work at," Cliff stated as his hand slid up her leg, so slowly she almost missed it, except the motion was slowly pushing the hem of her dress up.

"I will look into your claims of who you are." Kirk pulled out his phone.

"Clifton Scott V, look me up. Old number IV was recently talking about a gym that needed some more funding. I think I could make that dry up quickly, which means they would have to look elsewhere for that money. What department are you in again? Literature or children's literature? I'd like to be prepared when I talk to the dean."

Kirk's hand was shaking as he held his phone before pocketing it when he couldn't even get it open. "I am still looking into it."

"Tomorrow, I think I'll just go and talk to the dean about any previous complaints about you. Take a look at the file. And if by chance there isn't a file, I think we should talk to some of the women who have worked for you in the last few years. There might be some stories there. I think the dean will be interested enough to make some of the calls himself." Cliff's thumb brushed her core. It was covered by a thin layer of fabric, and Mabel was sure he could feel how wet she was.

"You are an ass!" Kirk got up and threw his napkin on the table.

"No, I'm a Scott. Very close though." Cliff grinned at him as they watched him scurry out of the restaurant.

Cliff turned to Mabel without moving his hand, and said, "You do look beautiful in that dress. No wonder he was crazy for you. I'd be crazy for you also."

"Holy shit, he almost ran out of here! What did you say?" Lucy hurried over to the table, interrupting the sizzling moment between them. At her words, Cliff's hand instantly left Mable's body, reminding her that everything that just happened was pretend.

"Just about the email and how Maby will go to the dean if there are any more issues. I think he at least believes we're engaged." Cliff told the lie with an ease Mabel wished she could. She couldn't tell her twin the truth about Cliff's real threat without telling her who he really was, or who his family was.

"Engaged? I thought dating would be enough." Lucy looked at them.

"I thought he needed to know that Mabel was never going to be available. If I could've said we were married, I would have." Cliff put his arm around Mabel, the one that had just been touching her intimately. Though this seemed riskier than that had because Lucy was watching them.

"I told you Cliff would be able to help," Lucy said to Mabel with a triumphant smile.

"I shouldn't have doubted him." What she should have done was look up his family. After she had gotten home, she hadn't wanted to because she had wanted to stop thinking about him. But it seemed that they had more than just money; they had a lot of power behind their name when they wanted to use it. She wondered what else they had built or financed over the years.

"I think we should go out and celebrate!" Lucy smiled and got up, waving off the waitress that was suddenly heading their way.

"Me too, fiancée," Cliff whispered to her. Getting up, he tossed a few bills on the table. With one look, Mabel knew they were hundred-dollar bills. All for a meal they hadn't even ordered yet.

Mabel followed Cliff and Lucy from the room as a battle waged in her mind. Half of her wanted to spend more time with Cliff, and the other half didn't want to take the risk of drinking tonight. The stress of the day would make her want to toss a few more back than she should, and then where would she be?

On the street, Lucy and Cliff were chatting about something and laughing, clearly ready to start the evening. Mabel felt out of place. Even if she loved spending time with both of them, she didn't feel like being a third wheel.

"You two go. I have a lot of work to do for the morning," she lied. She had nothing to do; her lesson plan was done. Now she just had to wait for the semester to start.

"Come on, Maby, don't be a spoilsport. It'll be fun." Lucy stated.

"I know, I'm just not up for it tonight. How about Friday?" she asked, knowing Lucy would forget by then or would have made other plans.

"Yes, Friday," Lucy said with excitement.

"Are you sure, Maby?" Cliff asked.

"Yes, you two have fun. Don't even think about me."

"We won't," Lucy called as she pulled Cliff away from her.

"I know," Mabel whispered as she turned and headed for her own vehicle parked down the street. Climbing in, she just sat there for a while, letting the loneliness creep in. Yes, it was her fault that she was alone, but it was nothing on the loneliness she had felt in that hospital bed years before.

Cliff was better off with Lucy anyway. They were friends and would be friends for a long time unless Lucy found out about them. Then Lucy would be mad at them both, and Mabel was sure Lucy would pick Cliff over her. Then she would be alone again. She would have lost them both .

CHAPTER TWENTY-FOUR

WALKING AWAY from Mabel in front of the restaurant had been the hardest thing he had done since letting her go at the airport. Why was saying goodbye to this woman so hard? Maybe if he knew when he was going to see her next, it would help. Maybe if he could have said more than a goodbye, been able to kiss her, or told Lucy he wanted to go where Mabel was going.

Seeing her had been even more difficult today after his conversation with his mom the day before. As always, his mom was his rock, and she let him talk about the woman he had fallen for who was so different than him. He had even admitted to calling his dad for a job so that he could be more than a bartender for Mabel. But in the end, the talk hadn't changed anything. Mabel was out of his league.

"For this being a celebration, you're sure a sad sack," Lucy said from beside him.

"Sorry, just hate wearing suits." He pulled off the tie, blaming his mood on the formal clothing and not the fact that he was constantly missing Mabel.

"But you look hot in a suit. Even Maby thought so."

Even hearing Lucy talk about Mabel made him miss her more. Every time he was with her, it made him hate being without her more.

When Lucy had called and said that Mabel was in trouble, he knew he would do whatever it took to help her. For Lucy and for Mabel. That some guy was using her job as leverage for her to date him, or more, made him see red. There was no way he would not be at the restaurant; he wouldn't let that creep have more than a minute alone with his woman. His woman, who wanted him to be more than he was.

"Luce, do you think I'm wasting my life as a bartender?" He truly wanted to know what she thought. She was his best friend. Even though she had goals, he didn't, except his sudden new goal of wanting to better himself for her sister.

"Why? You saved a life this week. That's not wasting." Somehow, she had heard about that. Cliff supposed it wasn't a secret, and if she had gone to the bar, they would have told her. But he hadn't wanted her to know, to see him as more than a bartender. He didn't want Lucy to suddenly be his friend because of who his family was.

"I'm serious."

"I don't know. Do you enjoy it?"

"Sometimes." He toyed with his beer bottle.

"Do you dream about doing something else?"

"Sometimes," he said, not looking up at her. Cliff did have dreams, and they all centered on her sister.

"You're making this hard. Sometimes? Cliff, if you enjoy it, then do it. I love catering. I can't see myself doing anything else. It makes me happy. But I have to clean offices right now because we aren't making enough yet. But one day, we will, and then it'll all be worth it. And I won't have to have a side hustle." Lucy always made her life seem so easy. She never mentioned her struggles or things that weren't so rosy in her life.

"Do you think I could sell stuff?" he asked as their second round of drinks finally showed up.

"Yes, you can sell anything. You could be a con man, you're so good. I mean, look at tonight! You made Kirk believe you were in love with Maby and that you could end his career." Lucy giggled and finished off her first drink even as she pulled the second to her.

Looking into his beer bottle, he knew neither of those were bluffs; they were both true. Con men weren't supposed to believe the bluff. Suddenly, he wanted the bluff so bad. He wanted to be the man who could save Mabel every time she needed saving, or just be there to know when she needed saving.

"Tonight was different. Tonight was to save Maby." Mabel didn't need him to save her because Mabel wasn't the type that needed saving.

"Maby could have handled herself, but sometimes, she needs someone to help her out. She really pushes herself to be perfect, but there are chips every now and then. She needs help polishing those chips so she can remain perfect." She poked at the ice in her glass.

"Name a chip." He leaned toward her because they were finally talking about Mabel. He wanted to learn more about what made her who she was.

"She likes to tell people that she was the closest to Dad, that they would talk and that's why she likes literature. But in reality, she talked, and he didn't listen. He never talked back to her. He couldn't tell us apart, ever." She fished out an ice cube and popped it in her mouth.

"Ever? You were his kids." Cliff didn't know many people who couldn't tell the twin sisters apart. Even people at the bar could

"He didn't care enough to know that there were differences. It's why we always say we don't look alike. Because if you look close enough to tell us apart, then we know you care." She shrugged, her words saying as much about Lucy as it did about Mabel, maybe more.

"I can tell you apart." He grinned at her. Oddly, he could from the beginning. Unless one of them was trying to fool him into believing they were the other, he could tell them apart.

"I know. That's what makes you so special. How was the big smooch? You went above and beyond on that one. For a minute, I thought you were a couple. I mean tongue, Cliff? I was sure she would slap you afterward." Lucy finally took a drink and raised her eyebrows

"Just my acting skills paying off," he lied. The kiss had all been real. Too real, and he wanted those moments back.

"You had me convinced. But she's way out of your league, Cliff. Like galaxies away." Lucy broke down laughing at her description of her double. Before he could answer, his attention turned to the crowd that had formed since they had arrived. This was a new bar, and they didn't see anyone they knew. And maybe that was for the best; a change of scenery was good.

Lucy was wasted by the time she was ready to head home, but Cliff had slowed his drinking after the first one since he knew he'd be driving. Not being a few blocks from the bar was a pain. Cliff had realized early on that Lucy wouldn't be able to get herself home when it was time, so he let her celebrate.

Dropping her off in her bedroom, he ignored her drunken pleas for him to stay. At this point, he needed to be away from both Lovely twins, so he could think. They were making him want things he had never wanted before, things that he had been running from for years.

CHAPTER TWENTY-FIVE

Mabel had kept her head down for over a week. Except for a few sightings, she hadn't crossed paths with Lucy, and there had been no sightings of Cliff at all. Not once did he sneak into her room at night. She wished she hadn't spent so much time at work

On a positive note, Kirk Langley hadn't come into work all week, and by Friday, there were rumors he wouldn't be returning. There was talk that he had found a job on the West Coast somewhere.

At this point, she had no idea if Cliff had actually gone to the dean or if just the threat of it was enough to send Kirk running. But it didn't matter because he was gone, hopefully forever. She just wished she had handled it herself.

It was quiet when Mabel walked into the Lovely house that Friday night. The TV wasn't on, and the house was almost completely dark, which was just fine with her. Nobody around meant she wouldn't have to make up an excuse for not going out on the town on a Friday night again.

Up the stairs, she nearly ran into Lucy coming out of her room. She was in jean shorts and a tank top, a nod to the hot, humid weather. Mabel's own slacks and short sleeve blouse were not.

"Maby, we have to go out." Lucy grabbed her around the waist to turn her around to go back down the stairs, backpack and all.

"No, I'm tired." She resisted her sister's movements.

"Too bad. We need to go out and drink. We still have to celebrate my plan that saved your job."

"How about tomorrow?" Mabel pushed.

"Nope, today," Lucy insisted.

"I need to change." Mabel could tell she was losing the battle, but there was no way she was going out in her work clothes.

"I'll help. I'll pick out what you are going to wear; dress you all sexy." Lucy let her go and followed her into her bedroom.

"I can pick out what I'm going to wear," she argued, dropping her bag on the desk.

"Nope, me." Lucy pulled open her closet door and looked inside as if she didn't know most of what was in there. "What in here could possibly make Maby look sexy?"

Mabel just sat on her bed. There was no use in saying no to Lucy. Once the woman got something in her head, there was no stopping her. You just had to let it happen.

"I'm thinking red and tight." Lucy pulled out a dress and waved a hand over it.

The last time Harper had worn that dress, she had made her boyfriend take her to one of the most expensive restaurants in town. She'd had him drooling over her throughout the entire meal, only to dump him as they left. He had been cheating on her. Mabel had never worn the dress again and didn't know why it was still in her closet.

"I am not wearing that. You're wearing shorts." Mabel leaned against the headboard.

"Yes, you are, because you need to find a man. It's been ages since you've had a man in your life. You need to find a guy." Lucy tossed the dress at her, and it landed on the edge of the bed. Mabel didn't move to get it.

"You don't have a man in your life," Mabel pointed out.

"I'm just coming off a relationship. I need my freedom for a while."

"Maybe I should be focusing on my career."

"Nope, your career is going fine, now. Do I hear a 'thank you'?" She picked up the dress and looked at it again.

"Thank you, Lucy. Now, how is your career going?" she asked as Lucy put the dress back in the closet.

"I don't have a career, just jobs." She didn't look away from the clothes in the closet.

"Catering is a career."

"For Harper, not for me. I am just her helper. I love my job, but it'll never be like Harper. She's the chef."

"It hasn't been like that for a while, Lucy. You're more like her partner now. Does she tell you that you're just a helper?" Mabel wondered if it was more than just Harper being controlling. That maybe Harper wasn't giving their sister a chance to grow.

"We don't talk about it. I think she likes having me around, and I like catering. I'm even kind of good at it. Not as good as her, but pretty good." Lucy started going through her drawers.

"Does she let you do more than cook and clean up?"

"Not really, but you know Harper. Control is her middle name." She pulled out a white shirt and tossed it at Mabel.

"Do you want to help more in the business? Like with the books?" She picked up the shirt and looked at it.

"No, I'm awful at math. You know that. Best to let Harper worry about that." She pulled out a white skirt from another drawer and tossed it her way.

Shaking her head, Mabel tossed the skirt back at her sister, who took and put it back in the drawer, pulling out a moss green one instead. "Don't you want to try it?"

"No, I don't like the business side. I like the cooking side, Maby. I'm good at the cooking side."

"But you could be good at the other side also."

"No, I didn't make it through tenth-grade math. No way could I manage business math."

"If you wanted to, I'm sure you could do it." Mabel pushed, hoping that her sister would confide in her. She wanted Lucy to tell her her secret, so Mabel could help her. Unless Lucy admitted it, Mabel couldn't tell her that she knew.

"But I don't. I like just doing what I do. No pressure, no stress. I like to leave all that to Harper. She lives for it." Which was a fact; Harper wasn't actually happy unless there was a deadline and things to do.

"Okay. So, what are we doing tonight?" Mabel changed the subject as she changed her blouse for the white one.

"We're going to the Grog and then off to Agatha's jazz place later since she doesn't start until after eleven." Lucy jumped off the bed, ready for the night to begin.

"If we make it that long." Mabel hated that there was so much time between now and the end of the night.

"We will. I know we will. I'm buying tonight—I promised Cliff." Lucy grabbed her sandals and held them out as Mabel put on the skirt.

"Is Cliff going?" Her hands shook as she pulled on the skirt, hating that just his name could get this kind of reaction from her.

"Yes, Maby. Can you two at least get along for a night for me? Then you can go back to not liking each other. Or maybe not. Maybe you'll find out that he's as much fun as I think he is. Though I can't actually see you two as friends since you are so different."

"What if I fall for him?" Mabel couldn't help but ask.

"You can't. He's mine. I have first dibs on him." Lucy headed out the door for the hallway.

"I thought you didn't like him that way?" Mabel could barely get the words out fast enough as she tried to catch up.

Had Mabel read her sister wrong this entire time? Had she wanted Cliff? Why wouldn't she just say that before? Why hadn't Mabel just asked her outright before?

"I don't, but if he's going to like one of us, it'll be me. And I really don't think you two would last longer than a week. I know you both best, and you two wouldn't last, which is why I never tried to set you up. That, and he's *so* not your type," Lucy said, leading the way down the steps.

"You're right." Mabel's heart sank as she admitted what was in the back of her mind since Florida. They were too different to make it work. At this point in her life, she wasn't changing for a man, and she knew it wasn't fair for her to ask him to either.

"I know, I always am." Lucy opened the door into the sweltering heat and humidity and led them to one of the red Jeeps in the yard.

The jazz bar was a few miles away, so they needed to drive, which meant Mabel could pull the designated driver card if she needed it. And she was sure she would need it.

Since the Grog was only three blocks away, they were entering the bar before Mabel had time to prepare herself to see Cliff again. It wasn't long enough. Instantly, she spotted them him at the bar. He was in white shorts and a navy-blue polo shirt. Unable to stop her feet from moving toward him, she almost beat Lucy to his side.

Lucy gave him a side hug and turned her attention to the bartender behind the bar, leaving Mabel and Cliff to look over each other at their leisure.

"You look gorgeous tonight, Maby." His words were said low, and he started to reach his hand out to her but dropped it.

"Not bad yourself, Cliff." Mabel was glad she had let her sister dress her but knew this night had been a mistake, and not because she would be drinking. Not drinking wasn't going to be as difficult as not touching Cliff.

"Here, Maby." Lucy turned and handed her a drink, not noticing anything between her friend and sister.

Taking the drink, she looked around for a table because she couldn't stand anymore. All she wanted to do was lean into Cliff's strength. Pointing at one, she led the way, not caring if they were following.

After sliding into the booth, she set her glass down, still undrunk, though she had managed to spill a bit on the walk over. It was going to be a long night.

"Have you had any more issues at work, Maby?" Cliff slid in across from her.

"No. I'm pretty sure Langley has left. Thank you," was all she could say. She wanted to touch his hands that were resting on the table.

"That's good. I hope someone called the dean the next morning, making it impossible for him to come back," Cliff stated cryptically, but Mabel knew he had made the call.

"Cliff was amazing that night." Lucy slid in next to Cliff and moved his arm until it was around her shoulder. Like they were a couple.

"Yes, he was. I don't know what I would have done without him," Maby replied, looking away from them. Though they had always been touchy-feely, their affection was something she couldn't watch tonight.

"At least we don't have to find out. Cliff is here to stay," Lucy said, bringing Mabel's attention back to them as Lucy leaned across the table. "P.S., he saved the life of a college girl this week; a true lifesaver."

"What happened?" she asked Cliff, her attention off Lucy for a moment.

"Just a bad reaction to drugs and alcohol," he said quietly, his eyes on her.

"Oh," was all she could say around the lump in her throat.

CHAPTER TWENTY-SIX

CLIFF WATCHED Mabel's smile vanish at his words. She knew exactly how he knew what the warning signs were; she had told him. It would be the perfect time for Mabel to tell her sister everything, but Mabel just took a very small sip of her drink and set it back down. So far, she hadn't actually taken a full drink of the beverage in front of her.

Lucy was watching the band as they set up their instruments, and Cliff switched his and Mabel's drinks, leaving her with a nearly empty glass and him a completely full one. As long as they were together tonight, he would cover for her, not letting Lucy know what was happening.

"Can you believe he did that? I've worked in bars for years and would never have picked up on the fact that something like that was happening. But Cliff did," Lucy boasted for her friend.

"I can believe it. Bartending is his calling," Mabel said, taking another tiny sip from the nearly empty glass.

"Not really my calling, Maby," he mumbled. He hated when people said that. Bartending was a job, not a career. Instead of saying more, he took a big drink of what had been her beverage.

Cliff hated how much he missed talking to her. Sure, he missed her body since they had returned from Florida, but he'd had that. It was talking to her that they hadn't done since getting back. Tiny stolen words were not enough; he wanted to talk to her about everything and nothing.

Like this morning when his dad had called him, this time not offering him a job that Clifton IV wanted his son to have, but a job that Cliff might actually want to do. Oddly, Mabel had been right about his interests, and he wanted to tell her that. The job was head of the philanthropy division of the company. It seemed that the long-time chair of the division was looking to retire but didn't want to leave the company without anyone in the position. So, starting on Monday, Cliff was going to give it a try and see how he liked it.

"Harper!" Lucy yelled from beside him as she started waving franticly at the door.

Mabel turned toward the door to find where her oldest sister in the crowd. When she turned back to him, she caught his eye and whispered a thank you. Smiling at her, he nodded and mouthed, "Miss you."

Instantly, he regretted his admission, and even more so when he saw Harper looking right at him, her eyes swinging from him to Mabel and back again. Without a word, Harper took his drink from his hand and downed the rest of it before sitting down beside Mabel in the booth, pushing her hard as she did it.

"Really!" Harper demanded at the table when the alcohol was gone.

"How is Harper?" he asked the blonde. She was dressed more relaxed than the twins tonight. Her blue shirt said Kantaty, which was supposed to read Kentucky. Whichever sister who wound up wearing it always thought it should say Kantity.

"Wondering what's going on?" Harper didn't answer the question but shot him daggers instead. She knew something was up and wasn't pleased. Cliff wondered if this was a prequel to how Lucy would react.

"We're having a night on the town to celebrate Maby's boss getting what he deserved." Lucy grinned at her older sister, missing the undertones of the conversation.

"The one you fucked?" Harper asked, knowing it was a sore spot for the twins. But Harper liked to poke when she could. Since she had no idea who was in the wrong over the entire Cliff thing, she might as well poke everyone.

"I did not! He was a creep and was making Maby's life miserable. But Cliff helped us trick him into leaving," Lucy summed it up but missed quite a bit of the story.

"Cliff, huh?" Harper turned to Maby, not even asking about the story.

Mabel looked like she was a fly trapped in Harper's web, and Cliff had no idea how she was going to get out of this one. Harper was a notorious interrogator in the family; she could make anyone talk.

"Yes, he helped me out that day." Mabel pushed her empty glass to the center of the table.

"I bet." Harper folded her arms. "Bathroom, Maby. Now."

Before Mabel could protest, Harper grabbed her arm and pulled her from the booth and dragged her from the table. Lucy was looking around the bar and not paying much attention to her sisters. To her, they had done nothing strange. Over the last year, he had learned the Lovelys acted strange all the time. It was when they were acting normal that you had to worry.

"There's nobody here," Lucy stated, her eyes darting around the room.

"Who are you looking for?" he demanded, wondering if she was actually over Kevin. Since returning, he had been so focused on Mabel he hadn't had time to think about Lucy and her ex.

Lucy gave a laugh. "Don't worry, I'm completely over Kevin."

Her voice didn't match her words; she was just telling him what he wanted to hear. Looking around the bar himself, he was happy he didn't see the loser.

Cliff watched as Harper came back to the table without Mabel. With a fake smile, she slid into the booth across from them again. "Maby's freshening up. What are you two chitchatting about?" She used finger quotes as she said it, leaving Cliff to wonder exactly what that meant.

"Nothing. Cliff's just being a jerk." Lucy pushed him away from her a little.

"You have no idea," Harper stated and grabbed Lucy's drink and finished it off.

Before Lucy could ask her to explain, the waitress came to their table and took drink orders all around. By the time all three had ordered, Mabel was walking back to the table. Looking at her closely, he couldn't see any damage to her, no black eyes or bruises. Both of which he had seen at least one of the sisters sporting over the last few months. Her eye wasn't even bruised from the weekend.

She pushed her way into the booth next to Harper again but didn't meet his eyes. That alone told him that Harper now knew and that their secret wasn't going to last long.

"How's work going, Harper?" he asked the blonde since she was giving him the stink eye anyway.

"Great, we have around thee bookings a week for the next month with the possibility of getting more. I think we're finally getting noticed. Tomorrow night we have the Mallory/Davis Wedding down-town. That one is big money. It's at the Jay, have you heard of it?" she asked.

He was sure both her sisters were aware of the locale. She would have already talked about the venue over and over since she learned about it. Cliff knew about it because it was one of his father's favorite places to rent for events, including his third wedding reception, and possibly his fourth.

"Never heard of it." He leaned back and looked around the bar.

"Because you have no class, Cliff. It takes deep pockets to rent the Jay and just as deep to be invited there. We might need you to be a waiter since we can't bring Buzz anymore." Harper stopped talking as the waitress brought their drinks, including one for Mabel, which she just toyed with.

"What did Buzz do?" he asked, though he was well aware of her makeout session with the groom at their last engagement party. Things like that put you on notice with Harper Lovely.

"Never mind what she did. What matters is that she won't do it again," Harper assured him.

"How about the office gig?" he asked since she, like Lucy, had a second job. Hers was not cleaning offices but a personal assistant to a CEO somewhere downtown. Weird hours, but she seemed to keep the job.

"Shit, Cliff. It's shit. I don't want to talk about it." Harper never did. It was an easy way to shut her up, which was needed sometimes. Like now.

"*Shit*," Lucy hissed and scrunched down in the booth beside him.

Looking around, he saw Kevin walk into the bar with a redhead on his arm. He was either done with Beth, or he was cheating on her. Either one was a possibility with him.

Shaking his head at Lucy's reaction, he knew she wasn't over the ass. Her curse had sounded mad, but her eyes were on the man, and she couldn't look away.

"We're leaving," he stated. No need to let Lucy stay and somehow get stuck on him again. Grabbing Lucy's arm, Cliff dragged her from the booth, much like how Harper had with Mabel not that long before.

Mabel looked around the bar and groaned when she saw Kevin.

"Once your drinks are done, come to the Fish and meet us there," he told her, hating that he was leaving her with full drinks on the table, but he had to get Lucy out of here before Kevin did something to hurt her. Hopefully, Mabel could put up with Harper alone because he wouldn't be able to help her until they met up at the next bar.

CHAPTER TWENTY-SEVEN

Saturday morning reminded Mabel why she didn't drink anymore; her head was killing her. After Harper had spent time grilling her about her and Cliff—what had actually happened between them and what was going on now—her sister had gotten bored, and Harper had gone on and on about other jobs she would be good at. The list included parole officer and mistress, both of which Harper would probably be better at than her current job as a personal assistant since her ability to take orders was a bit lacking.

Once they had met up with Lucy and Cliff at the Fish where Agatha worked, Harper was already drunk, and Mabel had more then she usually liked—way more. Which was why she hadn't even ordered a drink at the new bar. Luckily, nobody even noticed because the cravings were starting to surface the longer they were out.

Just after midnight, Mabel decided to take Harper home, and Agatha, who had just been fired, had offered to drive. To be honest, their sister had looked miserable working at the jazz bar. The bonus was that they had a sober driver to get them home. Just as Agatha was dropping them off at the house, she got a call from Lucy to come back and get them also.

Twenty minutes of tossing and turning, thinking over the night, she heard Cliff trying to guide the not-at-all sober and singing Lucy into her room. Whether he stayed with her or not, Mabel had no idea. She hadn't heard him leave, which left her lying in bed, wondering if Harper was right: had she had cross a line with Cliff? It was a line that shouldn't have been crossed if he was still willing to sleep with her sister.

After tossing and turning for hours, she finally fell asleep. But it was a short night because it was still dark when Harper's mixer woke her up. Heading down to the kitchen, she opted not to change from her lounge pants and T-shirt because the couch was going to be her home for today after last night.

Walking into the kitchen, she was surprised that both Lucy and Harper were awake and getting things ready for the usual weekend breakfast. It was sometimes the only time in the week that the entire family got together, and today was going to be no different.

"Morning," she called to the two discussing the menu for something happening this week, just shop talk for the caterers.

"Morning, Maby. Did you sleep well?" Harper asked. She looked just as bright-eyed as Lucy. Was Mabel the only one who couldn't handle their liquor? How was neither of them hungover?

"I did. How are you two not hungover?" she demanded, sitting at the island and watching the two move around the kitchen.

"I barely drank," Harper stated, as if she hadn't had at least nine drinks the night before, possibly more. Mabel had lost count about the time Cliff and Lucy had left because she had polished off the ones they had left behind.

"You ended the night doing shots!" Mabel stated in disbelief.

Lucy started to sing, "Tequila makes her clothes fall off."

"I kept them on!" Harper argued, then turned to Mabel all serious, "Maby, I might have spilled something on your shirt."

Mabel shook her head. Harper had insisted that she needed to wear Mabel's white shirt soon after getting to the Fish, and they had switched tops. Sadly, Harper had forgotten the fact that she was braless until she had her shirt off, a fact that had only made her laugh the night before. Now it seemed she barely remembered it happening. But then again, flashing a bar wasn't something new to her.

"You can get the stain out," Mabel told her. Her stain, her responsibility.

"I will have Mom do it," Harper said dismissively.

"Do what?" said the woman herself as she came into the kitchen. Sera was already dressed or still dressed, in black leggings and a bright yellow T-shirt that said Bastan.

"Mabel's shirt got a little tomato juice on it at the jazz place last night. I was wearing it, so I have to clean it," Harper complained, or more like whined.

"Just toss it in your dirty clothes. I'm doing laundry today. I always add bleach to the white load. Gets all your stains out, Harps." Sera sat down next to Mabel and gave her a side hug.

"Thanks, Mom." Harper pulled out a pan with chicken swimming in a thick sauce from the oven.

"How was the Fish?" Sera asked as she leaned close enough to the pan that Harper had to push her away from it.

"Ag got fired, like right away," Lucy explained, handing Sera and Mabel plates.

"Why?" Sera asked.

Lucy shrugged. "I didn't see, and she didn't say."

"I should go talk to her." Sera set down her plate and started to get up.

"Her door is shut." Buzz came into the room, catching the end of the conversation.

Everyone knew that a shut door meant you didn't go in. Especially Agatha's. Usually, it also meant there was company, male-type company.

"Well, good for her," Sera said, holding up her plate for some chicken. Nobody even noticed that she was happy her daughter might be getting lucky in the same house she was in, but that was what it was like being a Lovely.

"You can pretend to think we're innocent," Mabel tried to sound hurt, but didn't make it through the last word before breaking down laughing. Which only caused her mom to give her an eye roll as chicken was added to her plate.

"Why start now? I know for a fact that two of you were having sex before I even became part of your family." Sera happily took her plate.

"Holy fuck! Mabel Lucie Atwell Lovely, you play all innocent," Harper stated loudly and glared at Mabel.

"Why do you even think it's me?" she demanded, setting down her plate, no longer as hungry as she had been.

"Because I was innocent as the driven snow when she showed up, and Buzz and Agatha," she pointed at Buzz alone, "were ten and eleven. So, she must mean you and Lucy."

"This really isn't all that important," Mabel stated lamely, then changed topics quickly, "Climate change, now that is important.

"Did you have sex before me?" Lucy ignored Mabel and took her plate from her.

"I have no idea," Mabel said honestly, eyeing the plate.

"Can your sex life get anymore sordid, Maby?" Harper asked, waving a spatula at her, sauce splattering everything.

"Are we talking about Cliff then?" Agatha walked into the room, still in what she had worn the night before, but her hair was messed up a little.

All conversation stopped and there was an audible gasp. It wasn't Mabel who'd gasped, but she wished it had been her. Instead, she was frozen in place.

"What about Cliff?" Lucy demanded, still holding her baked goods.

The room went completely silent. Mabel knew that if anyone could have left, they would have, instantly.

"What about Cliff? And Maby? And sex?" Her eyes went right to Mabel. "Did you have sex with Cliff?"

"Agatha has no idea what we were talking about, Lucy," Mabel stated, though everyone else was looking at her, staring at her.

Lucy stared at her also, but Mabel held her glare. This wasn't their first staring contest, and it wouldn't be their last. With a curse,

Lucy slammed the hot pan in her hands down on the counter and headed for the stairway, throwing her oven mitts on the floor as she went.

"Oh fuck." Mabel was off the stool and following her sister, who was now running up the stairs. Realizing Cliff must be still in her room, she hurried to catch her sister before she got to her room. "Luce, stop."

"No fucking way," Lucy called over her shoulder and pushed her way into her room. Mabel right behind her.

Cliff was sitting on the edge of the bed in just his shorts and with one sock on and one sock off when they barged in. Cliff looked up at them, and Mabel knew he knew the jig was up right away. Even before Lucy opened her mouth.

"Have you been fucking my sister?" Lucy demanded, stomping right up to him and grabbing the sock from his hand. She whacked him across the face with it.

"Lucy, I can explain," Cliff stated calmly, more calmly then Mabel felt.

"You are going to explain to me what?" she asked in angry amusement. "How sex works or how you're having sex with my sister?"

"Lucy, we didn't plan for this to happen," Mabel said from the door.

"How long has this been going on? I told you to stay away from my sisters. She's not some plaything, Cliff. She isn't like that." She punctuated each question with a smack of the sock.

"I know, Lucy," he stated lamely.

"You don't know anything, Cliff. Get out of my house." Lucy let go of the sock and turned her back on him. Her body was tense as she looked out the window with her arms folded tight to her chest.

Reluctantly, Cliff got up from the bed, grabbed his shirt, and almost said something to Lucy, but he must have decided against it. Turning from her, he looked at Mabel in the doorway, then walked past her and out the hallway. Silently, he walked past the rest of the Lovely sisters as they had all followed them up the stairs.

"Lucy ..." Mabel started, though she had no idea what she was going to say. She had betrayed her sister as much as Cliff had. Maybe even more.

"Shut up, Mabel! Do you know what's worse than me possibly sleeping with your boss? You fucking my best friend behind my back!"

"I'm sorry, Lucy."

"Was it out of spite? Because you thought I slept with that creep you worked for? A revenge screw?" Lucy hissed.

Her words hit home. It really did look like that was Mabel's motivation, though it never had been. It was only just her being horny, and him being there. Never once was it about getting back at Lucy.

"No, it just happened. I'm sorry."

"No, you're not. If you were sorry, you would have told me about it. Instead, you lied to me. On top of that, everyone already knew! I was the only one who didn't know. We're twins, I should know," Lucy whispered.

"I …" Mabel tried but didn't know what to say. But Lucy was right, completely right. Mabel had no excuse for hiding it from her and now felt like she had ruined everything. Not only her sister's friendship with Cliff but also her friendship with her twin.

Lucy turned to her and stated calmly, "You know what? You can leave my house too."

"I live here. Where would I go?" she asked because she had no place else.

"Go wherever you went when you were gone for that week. You seemed to enjoy not being here."

"But …" How could she tell Lucy that she had been with Cliff on Lucy's vacation? That wasn't even an option anymore.

"Go then, just go." Lucy pushed her out of her room and slammed the door in her face.

"Sorry, Maby." Agatha sounded as if she meant it.

"It was going to come out eventually." It wasn't Agatha's fault; it was Mabel's. She was the one who'd slept with Cliff, knowing her sister wouldn't like it. But it didn't make her feel any better about it.

"It'll blow over, Maby," Sera said, putting her arm around her.

Pushing away from her, Mabel tried to hold back the tears, but failed. "No, no it won't. I have to go."

Without another word, she walked past the same sisters Cliff had walked past a few minutes before. Down the stairs and out the door, she had no idea where she was going, and really, she didn't care. All she needed was to be away from everyone she loved; everyone she had hurt by her actions.

CHAPTER TWENTY-EIGHT

The Mallory/Davis wedding reception was in full swing when Cliff walked into the Jay. At first, nobody noticed him, but as he saw more and more familiar faces, he began to get confused looks, then waves, and even actual hellos. Stan Mallory, the bride's father, was one of his father's oldest frenemies. They both worked in banking, but Stan worked in one that had tried to buy some of Clifton IV's banks over the years. Not that his father hadn't done the same thing in the past, sometimes even successfully.

After saying a quick hello to the couple, he made sure his father wasn't actually present because there was a possibility that he was invited. Not seeing the old man, he headed for the kitchen to see Lucy. She was the only reason he was at the party.

In two days, he began his new career, and he wanted to tell Lucy about it himself. Sure, he could easily walk away from their friendship, and she would be none the wiser of who he was, but Lucy deserved better than that. All the Lovelys did.

The first dance was being called as he pushed his way into the kitchen, which, in contrast to the dining room, had all the lights on and was a perpetual beehive of activity.

Buzz was the first to notice him. "I don't think you really want to be here." It seemed Lucy's sisters had been forgiven, but Mabel was missing from the group. Everyone else was there.

"I just want to talk to Lucy for a minute. I knew she would be here tonight," he told the redhead.

"She's busy, and I can't spare her for a little talk," Harper said, not even turning to look at him. She was busy cutting huge slabs of cake in perfect lines.

"The party's almost over, Harper. Just a few minutes," he replied, even though Lucy was pouring champagne not three feet from her oldest sister. She was ignoring him.

"No can do. Busy," Harper nearly growled.

Over the last year, he had seen the sisters interact with each other in every way possible, except this. Never had he seen Harper's mama bear side. They would fight each other at the drop of a hat, even in public. But usually, they didn't fight with others until now. He was pretty sure that she wouldn't hesitate to punch him in the face or kick him in the balls for hurting her sister. Cliff felt like he deserved it for what he had done.

"Harper, it's up to Lucy," Sera stated from behind him. He hadn't thought she would be there. Since her engagement to Harrison, she wasn't working for the sisters like she used to. The man in her life was taking up all her time now, and she happily let him.

"She's busy, Mom," Harper turned her anger on the older woman.

"I can do it," Sera glared at Harper as she went and grabbed the champagne bottle from Lucy.

Lucy looked from Harper to Sera and then to him. He was sure she didn't want to talk to him, probably assuming he was gone for good. He should have been, except he couldn't leave Lucy like this. He was in love with her sister, and he had finally accepted that over the last dozen hours.

After leaving the Lovely house, he had headed for his own place. Brad was actually awake and alone, which was something Cliff hadn't seen in months. After telling him he was moving out, Cliff had left enough money to cover his half of the rent for a year or enough to buy drugs that would last Brad for a month. By lunch, he had rented a new place; a bigger one that was completely empty. It was closer to his new job and cost ten times what his last apartment did, but the view alone had been worth the price. A call to his mom had her getting the entire thing furnished by the end of the day. That it was Saturday hadn't mattered to her at all. Once a rich man's wife, she still had the ability and means to make things happen.

An hour ago, he stood in his fully furnished, high-rise apartment, missing the only important thing in his life: Mabel. Changing his entire life to be worthy of her was worth every step he was taking, but not having her with him left a hole in him he had no way to fill until she was there.

He had texted her to call him early in the day, but she had ignored him. The same way Lucy was ignoring him now, but the difference was that they were in the same room.

"Lucy, please. Five minutes," he begged.

"Get it over with, Luce. Now," Buzz said, pushing her sister his way.

"I'll give you five minutes, but I will never forgive you. Ever," Lucy stated reluctantly.

Grabbing her hand, he pulled her out a side door that led to a second smaller ballroom. It was mostly dark and silent except for the thumping from the DJ in the next room. Lucy shook off his hand and sat in one of the many chairs that were already set up for the next event.

"So, you think you can explain fucking my sister?" Lucy demanded, her fingers tapping on the tabletop.

Reaching into his pocket, he pulled out a fidget spinner and placed it on the table in front of her, setting it spinning as he sat down in the chair next to her. Her eyes were on the item, but she didn't pick it up.

Though she looked at it, she wasn't taking the piece offering. The spinners were everywhere in Lucy's life—something to do with her constantly moving fingers. And though she was tapping her fingers on her leg, which was also bouncing, she ignored the toy.

"It wasn't like that, Luce. I got to know her, and I found out I really like her. Yes, I know we don't have a lot in common, but our differences make us better together."

"When, Cliff? When did you get to know her? One night in a bar, and wham, you like her? It was only yesterday."

"In Florida. She came with me to Florida," Cliff admitted. Hadn't Mabel already told her what happened?

"Mabel has never been to Florida, Cliff." Grabbing the spinner, she gave it an angry spin.

"She pretended to be you when Kevin, Beth, and I went. She even pulled it off for an entire day."

"So, a few days in Florida, and now you like her. Do you love her?"

"Yes, I love her so much, it's sometimes hard to breathe without her," he admitted. It was time to lay all his cards on the table. Because if not now, then when?

"Mabel?" Lucy sounded incredulous. *"My Mabel?"*

"Mabel Lucie Lovely." He confirmed with a nod, saying her name out loud.

"You're not good enough for her. Have you met her? Her standards are like here." She waved her hand over her head, then dropped it to the floor. "And you are here."

Lifting her hand until it was about eye level, he said, "I'm closer to here. Not because of anything I've done, but my family has money."

"Money? As in money or *money*?" she asked, her brown eyes wide.

"More money than we know what to do with," he admitted.

"You have got to be kidding me! All this time you've had money, and you've been sponging off me? I have nothing! Well, I had a sister, but you took that also. Didn't you?"

"I didn't take anything from you," he insisted.

"Bull, Cliff. Your five minutes are up, so I'm leaving. I would suggest you go find someone else to trick into letting you into their lives because I'm done with you." She walked out of the ballroom but turned at the door for one last parting shot. "And leave my family alone. All of them."

Cliff was alone, sitting in an empty bathroom, hating himself for what he had done to his best friend. He hated that he had killed their friendship over a little sex and seriously wishing that sex hadn't turned to love.

CHAPTER TWENTY-NINE

EVERYONE WAS out of the house that night. The older sisters were at the wedding, and the little girls were with their father. Agatha had sent Mabel a text about the event hours before, probably in hopes she would show up and help with the event to get herself back in her sister's good graces. But Agatha was wrong; it just gave Mabel time to pack her stuff and get out of the house for a while, or forever.

Not that she even knew where she was going, just away from Lucy. With her door open, she could see into her sister's room. It was decorated in yellow, different from her own purple, but oddly similar. Neither room actually showed any personality of the occupants, not after Sera had them all decorated a decade ago.

It was going to be hard not living here with everyone and seeing her sisters, but she knew it was long past time to move on. Now she had a career and should have a life that didn't completely revolve around her sisters.

Pulling out more clothes and putting them into the suitcase, she tried not to cry. Mabel tried to remind herself this wasn't a sad thing. Moving on with one's life should be a happy event.

Her phone buzzed with a text, this time from Buzz asking if she was okay. Shooting off an "I'm fine" response, she paused to look at the one from earlier from Cliff. All it said was, "Call me," but she couldn't bring herself to do that.

What were they anyway? A casual vacation fling that they had been unable to stop once back from paradise? No, it had gone so far beyond that, far into feelings she didn't want to think about it.

"Running away?" Lucy asked from the doorway, scaring Mabel enough to drop her phone onto the purple rug at her feet.

"You scared me! Aren't you supposed to be working?"

"Harper let me off early. Something about having a bad attitude." Lucy walked into the room and grabbed Mabel's phone from the floor.

Trying to grab it away from her sister, Mabel failed. Her twin looked at the screen, seeing the unanswered text from Cliff. Then she looked at the one before it, the one that said "Goodnight, Maby." Maybe even the one before that one, the one that said, "Miss you." Not one was anything earth-shattering, but they were her connection to him. It was all Mable had at this point.

"I'll be gone in a minute." She picked up her pace, needing to get out of the house as soon as possible.

"Are you going to him?" Lucy demanded, blocking her path to the dresser.

Mable headed to the closet and grabbed a few items from in there. "Who?"

"As if, Mabel Lucie." Lucy blocked her way back to the suitcase.

"It's over, Lucy. It was never going to last anyway, so you can be happy with the fact that there is no Cliff and Maby and more. There never really was one." She clenched the clothes to her aching chest. Why was it so hard to admit it?

"So, my friends aren't good enough for Mabel Lucie Lovely? Just like I'm not good enough for you." Lucy grabbed the clothes from her arms and tossed them onto the floor.

Fighting back tears, Mabel stared at the clothes at her feet. "I have never, ever said that, Lucy."

"You didn't have to say it, Maby, I know it's how you feel. Always has been. I was never smart enough for you."

"You're as smart as I am, Lucy. Maybe even smarter," she insisted.

Lucy's eyes snapped hers instantly. "Whatever he told you is a lie. I am not and have never been … whatever he calls it."

"Dyslexic, Lucy. I have read and read about it, and I'm absolutely sure you have it. Every struggle you have points toward it."

"I am not disabled, Mabel!" Lucy turned from her and stomped to the bed, grabbed a pile of clothes from the suitcase, and threw them at Mabel.

"It's not a disability unless you let it be, Lucy. But if you let someone help you, you can learn to live with it. Not just ignore it completely." Mabel let the clothes fall to her feet. She didn't move.

"My life is perfectly fine. I have a job, hell, I have two. I even have friends, something you don't have a lot of," Lucy bit back at her.

"You're right. Your life is perfect. Or it will be again once I'm gone." She reached down and picked up the clothes. "Then you can be friends with Cliff again."

"I don't think that will be happening," Lucy scoffed but didn't block her as she put the armload of clothes into the suitcase again.

"Just forgive him. You can go back to being best buddies. I won't get in the way again. I'll stay away from you two. I did it before, and I can do it again. Hell, it'll be even easier because I won't even live here." She turned to get more stuff from her closet.

"When before?" Lucy grabbed her arm and spun her to face her.

"When you were friends, and I didn't go out with you anymore."

"You've never gone out with us. You stayed with the girls or had to study or used any other lame excuse so you could lord your teetotaling ways above us. So, when was before?" Lucy stood toe to toe with her, glaring.

"Never mind." Mabel pushed past Lucy and started to close the suitcase. If she needed more stuff, she could just buy it. She was done here.

"No, you never mind!" Lucy yelled at her, as if her statement made sense. "No more secrets!"

"Get out of my way!" She grabbed the suitcase but was blocked by her sister.

"No, you have to tell me. You have been avoiding him for how long? Months?" Lucy wouldn't move.

"Just drop it, Lucy Maud!"

"Months, probably since … you slept with him! When? Obviously, before you pretended to be me on vacation." How had her sister even figured it out?

"Just drop it."

"Does he think he slept with me? But it was really you?" Lucy accused her.

Feeling her cheeks burn with embarrassment or shame or both, Mabel dropped the suitcase at her feet. "That was an accident. Buzz was in my bed, so I went to yours. He came in, and it happened. I have no excuse."

"Does he know it was you?" Lucy demanded.

"I don't even know if he remembers it. He was drunk that night." She shrugged. After all the times they had been together, he'd never said anything.

"Oh, he remembers. He's been hinting about us hooking up for weeks now. Why didn't you say anything?"

"What do I say? 'Hey Lucy, I hooked up with your drinking buddy. I hope that's okay,'" she said mockingly.

"That would have been better than hiding it and sneaking around behind my back."

"Well, it won't happen again. It's all over. You can have your friend back, and I will be out of your hair. For good." She grabbed at the suitcase again.

"You think moving out will get you out of my life? We share a family, Maby! Clothes and makeup, too. Hell, we share a birthday. You think you can shake me so easily?"

"I think we need time apart for things to settle."

"You mean for me to get my shit together?" Lucy demanded.

"No, for me to," Mabel admitted, trying once again to leave the room.

"He isn't some lazy bartender, Maby. His family has money, so he can take care of you."

"I don't need taking care of," she stated defensively.

Lucy glared at her. "You know about the money?"

"Yes, he told me in Florida. I met his grandmother."

"So, you know everything. Was there anything you *didn't* talk about on your little vacation?" Lucy knocked the suitcase from her hand.

"Politics, religion, sports …" she trailed off.

"Literature?"

"Not really. I mean, it pops up in conversations at times." She shrugged and tried to reach of her case again.

Lucy pushed her chest, knocking her off balance. With a thud, she landed on the purple rug on her ass. Glaring up at her sister, she sat there and folded her arms since Lucy wasn't letting her leave anyway.

"You are so boring, Maby. Boring! How can Cliff even put up with you?"

"He doesn't, remember? We are not together."

"But you want to be."

"He was your friend first, Lucy. I'm stepping back."

"No, you're sitting on your ass. What do you think will happen if you keep sitting on your ass?"

"You won't knock me down again," she stated the obvious.

"You won't get hurt." Lucy kicked her foot lightly with hers.

"Same thing."

"Cliff's in love with you, Maby. I've never seen him in love before."

"He's not in love with me, Lucy. It was a fling that went on too long. We both know it was just that."

"You both are lying to yourselves about it. You two are so in love, you can't think straight."

"I am thinking perfectly fine."

"Letting go of the first guy you actually let yourself fall for is thinking perfectly straight? Until today I never thought you would find anyone good enough for you. But now I know it's Cliff. It has been Cliff and will always be Cliff. My Cliff!" Lucy crouched down and squeezed Mabel's face in her hands. "Are you going to take care of my Cliff? Treat him right?"

"Lucy, really?" Mabel didn't even know what she was asking of her sister. Was she forgiven? Was Lucy just giving up her rights to Cliff? Was she questioning the whole perfect thing?

"Now that I think about it." Lucy's butt landed on the floor, and she laughed. "Cliff is just me as a guy, so of course you would love him. I'm your other half, now Cliff will be yours as well. Bonus is I love you both."

"Lucy." She sighed.

"Not love-love, Mabel Lucie, just love. And your babies are going to be adorable. You must name one after me, maybe more than one." Lucy giggled.

Rolling her eyes at her twin, Mabel said, "We are not a couple, so no kids."

"Well, then we have to get you together. What's it going to take? Who's in the wrong here? I like to think it's him, but I know you way too much not to know it was you."

"Thanks, Luce."

"I'll locate him for you, and you can go get him." Lucy pulled out her phone.

"No, Lucy. It's not meant to be. I just have to—" She stopped when Lucy's phone made a pinging sound.

"Downtown?" Lucy questioned and turned her phone toward Mabel. It was blinking, and there was an address at the bottom that she couldn't not memorize.

"It's over, though, Luce." Her eyes were still on the phone and the blinking dot.

"You're absolutely right, Maby. You can't rush into this. You need a plan. Let me get everyone together, and we'll meet at the Grog and plan your next move. We'll call this operation 'Get Maby her man.' Or 'Cliff and Maby Part 2,' or 'Maby takes the stick out of her ass.'" Lucy stopped and laughed. "I like that one."

"Of course, you do." Maby tried not to smirk, but her sister was a character.

"I'll text everyone, and we'll get together and plan and get you smashed, so you tell us all the details of your sordid relationship with Cliff and who you had sex with before I did."

Ignoring the last comment, Mabel said, "Let's just stay here and do that. Minus the sex talking and most of the drinking."

"You need booze to get you to talk, Maby." Lucy was looking at her phone but not typing. Then she poked at it a few times, then looked again.

"I don't want to get drunk, Lucy."

"Posh, everyone wants to get drunk." She poked again.

"Let me rephrase it then. I can't get drunk. Not today, not tomorrow, not next week. It's why I don't go out with you guys all the time," she admitted, hating watching her sister's inability to type a text.

Lucy looked up her phone and stared at her. "You can be pompous with your work buddies, Mabel. But with us, you can be yourself."

"Lucy, I am an addict."

Lucy laughed and grabbed Mabel's cheeks again, squeezing them together. "And what exactly are you addicted to, Mabel Lucie Atwell Lovely?"

"Speed and alcohol, mostly in combination, but either can kill the cravings for a bit."

Lucy dropped her hands as her own face went pale. "You're serious!"

"Since college. It almost killed me once."

"As in dead?"

"As in a coma in the hospital for days and stern warnings not to try it again. That someone might not start CPR in time next time."

"What? When did ...? Where was ...? How didn't I ...?" Lucy couldn't get the questions out fast enough.

"I was living in the dorm. Dad was called but never came. I didn't want anyone to know. I'm perfect, after all." Mabel wiped a tear off Lucy's cheek.

"I almost lost you and I didn't even know it?" She threw herself into Mabel's arms, as if it had happened seconds before. That holding her tight would make it all go away.

"I'm okay now. I just have to stay away from alcohol and drugs. I want to go out with you guys, but I don't always trust myself."

"I made you drink last night." Lucy's eyes went wide with the realization.

"Cliff drank most of mine," she admitted.

"Cliff knows? Before me? You do love him!"

"I sort of do," she admitted, more to herself then to her sister. Somewhere in Florida, she had fallen for him, hard.

"Then no plan is needed. We need to get you together ASAP." Lucy jumped to her feet and pulled Mabel to hers. "Grab your phone. I'll send you a text with his address the moment I get it."

"Where will I be?" Mabel wanted to argue that the address was already on her sister's phone but felt that her sister had to do things her way. There was no pushing Lucy when she didn't want to be pushed.

"Driving to him!" Lucy dragged her down the stairs and pushed her out the front door and into the night. It was late already, but hopefully not too late for them.

CHAPTER THIRTY

CLIFF SHOULD HAVE BEEN CLEANING, except his apartment was in perfect order. There wasn't even a piece of paper lying around. He'd even been able to fit the entire pizza box in his fridge, so it wasn't lying on the counter or the coffee table or even on the floor.

Moments ago, Lucy had texted him saying they needed to talk and that she was coming to him, which was odd since she had only been to his old place once. But that once had been enough, she told him afterward. Hell, once had been too much for him too. That place had been disgusting.

Sitting on the couch, his leg bounced as bad as Lucy's always did. The nerves were going to kill him. He didn't know what Lucy wanted to talk about, but he hoped she had found a way to forgive him. He needed her on his side if he had any hope of winning Maby's heart.

After turning on the big screen TV, he immediately turned it off again. There was nothing that could take his mind off what was going to happen. He had no way to drown out his thoughts.

Leaning his head back against the couch, he stared at the white ceiling, planning. If he could get back on Lucy's good side, he could ask her to help him with Mabel. But he still wanted Lucy back as a friend, even if she forbid him from ever seeing Mabel again.

A knock on the door surprised him since he had sent the text a few minutes before, which was nowhere near enough time to get from the Lovely house. Jumping to his feet, he wondered who it could be. Only his mom knew where he was living now.

Swinging the door open, he saw Mabel leaning against the wall on the other side of the hallway. Her brown hair was loose and hanging over her shoulder, nearly obscuring the words on her purple shirt. He'd seen it before, and knew it said VVyomlny.

"Maby," he breathed. Not for an instant did he think it was Lucy—he knew the woman he loved from miles away.

"Cliff, nice place." She looked up and down the hallway but didn't move.

"You haven't even seen the apartment yet."

"The hallway is better than the dump I live in."

"I would move into the Lovely house in a heartbeat. I love that house."

"There are a lot of women there."

"I only want one of them." He rushed across the hallway and wrapped her in his arms, loving the feeling of her against him.

"I hope you mean me," she breathed as his mouth claimed her, telling her in no uncertain terms that it was.

Lifting her up, she wrapped her feet around his waist as he carried her into his apartment. Without taking his mouth from hers, he shut the door and leaned back against it.

Cliff leaned back slightly and pulled her shirt over her head as her fingers pulled his own shirt up. "I messed up, Maby, so much. Can you ever forgive me?"

Her hair tickled his hands that were holding her back, keeping her pressed to him. "Yes, because I messed up just as much. I should have just told Lucy what happened. Taken her anger then, not tried to sneak around and spend so much time away from you."

He kissed her again, loving that she tasted the same as always. Her hands were running over his body as if she had forgotten or was looking for changes since the last time they were together.

Pulling away again, he leaned his forehead against hers and said, "I got a new job. I want to be good enough for you. You deserve more than a bartender."

"Don't change for me. I love you as you. Living your best life!" She grinned, and he had to kiss her because he hadn't been able to for so long.

"It wasn't my best life because my best life is with you. And you're pushing me to be better."

"I liked you how you were."

"I didn't. I want to be better for you. Monday, I start in the philanthropy division of Scott Industries, working with giving away our money. Just like you said, I think I'll like it."

"You will love that. What a perfect job!" She gave him her half-smile, the one that drove him crazy.

"*You* are perfect. What do you think about being an executive's wife?"

"Wife?"

"You said yes on the plane, and I'm holding you to that." He started moving toward the couch but knew he couldn't put her down. He couldn't not hold her close.

"Cliff, that was to make Kevin jealous," she reminded him.

"Kevin wasn't looking," he admitted. "I just wanted to kiss you."

"You lied to me?" She pulled back and glared at him.

"You, love, were lying to me at the time. Since you weren't Lucy."

"Sorry about that." But she didn't seem so sorry about it right then.

"Don't do it again. Though, I don't think you can. Back then, I didn't know Mabel very well, but now I know everything about her." He unclasped her bra, and she let it fall to the ground.

"Everything?" She quirked an eyebrow at him.

"Probably not. I don't know how you got all your scars or why you're so much cuter then your twin," he whispered, unable to stop looking at her breasts, even after stubbing his toe on a chair and cursing.

"Nice answer. Lucy is the cause of almost all my scars, and I was born the cuter of the two of us." She kissed him lightly. "But I don't need your fancy apartment, Cliff. And to be honest, the money is maybe a little of a turn-off. I loved you as a broke bartender, so this new you might take some getting used to."

"I'm the same guy. I didn't change; just what I do and where I live," he said, shifting her in his arms.

She looked around the apartment, and he looked at her breasts. "It's okay."

"Could you live here?" he asked around a lump is his throat. He had never asked a woman to live with him, ever, but he didn't want to live anywhere Mabel didn't.

"And give up my room? Buzz has been measuring it for days. We can't let her win."

"I don't think I really want to move into the Lovely house, Maby."

"But you almost lived there with Lucy."

"But I never had sex with her, and I like making a lot of noise when I have sex with you."

"I don't make noise! I'm as silent as a church mouse."

"Kevin and Beth pounded on the walls more than once." He loved that she blushed at the memory.

Setting her down on her feet, he took her hands in his. "I have to confess something that I should have told you a long time ago, Mable. I hope you can forgive me. I hope that we can move past it."

"This sounds ominous." She crossed her arms over her bare chest.

"Okay, here it goes. Months ago, I was drunk and stayed with Lucy. She was drunk also, and we had sex. Lucy doesn't remember it happening, and it meant nothing, but it's been eating me alive. I should've told you before we had sex," he said the words with his eyes closed, then opened one to look at her. Her immediate reaction was to bite her lip.

"Do you compare us in your head?" she demanded.

"No, never. You're the only person I want to sleep with. That time was a mistake, a drunken mistake. I wish it had never happened, and it will never happen again. I will never sleep with anyone else ever again. Just you," he promised, knowing nobody else would compare to the woman right in front of him.

"You had better not." She let go of her chest and pushed his lightly.

"Pinky swear." He held out his littlest finger to her.

As her pinky linked with his, she said, "So, I have a confession. A while back, Buzz took my bed, and I slept in Lucy's because she was out. I might have had sex with you. I was sober, but a bit horny."

"It was you! The entire time! No wonder I was suddenly so attracted to you after never being attracted to Lucy." He stared at her, smirking.

"I didn't think you remembered. You were a bit of a lush, and you never said anything," Mabel said. They never really talked before the trip to Florida, but maybe if they had, this would have happened months before.

"I thought it was Lucy," he argued weakly.

"We do not look that much alike!" she grumbled like they both did with that answer.

"Virtual opposites." He grabbed her and spun her in a circle. Immediately, she wound herself around him again and laughed.

"Weird how twins can be like that," she said, running her hands through his hair. "Now take me to your bedroom and ravish me."

"Ravish?" He quirked an eyebrow at her.

"It means to seize and carry off by force and/or fill someone with intense delight. I want both." She took his cheeks in her hands and kissed him.

With a laugh, he headed for the bedroom to do her bidding.

CHAPTER THIRTY-ONE

TODAY WOULD BE a day for many firsts for Mabel. For starters, she had never brought anyone home, and two, she had never actually brought them home just in time for breakfast with her sisters. But Cliff had insisted on joining her for the meal because there was going to be some hard-core harassing going on. His protectiveness was cute.

His hand held hers tightly as they walked into the seemingly quiet house. Maybe nobody was up since they'd had breakfast together yesterday. Sometimes two days in a row didn't happen.

"Quit harping on me," Lucy said loudly from the kitchen, dispelling Mabel's hope that nobody would be home.

"Well, if you keep going back to him, I'm going to keep telling you he's a loser. You can do better." Harper was the one harping, as usual.

"Not today, Harper," Lucy stated.

"Every day, Lucy."

"Just shove it," Lucy said, followed by a slam of the oven door.

"Why must you start the day by fighting? Can't we just talk quietly until a decent hour?" Buzz yelled from the top of the stairs. Her bare legs were the first thing visible.

"To get your ass out of bed!" Harper yelled louder from the kitchen.

"You're here." Buzz, still in her pajamas, arrived at the bottom of the stairs. Her eyes went to Mabel, then to Cliff, and then to their joined hands. With a shrug, she stated, "I slept in your bed, and I'm going to kick you out. I know there's the five-day rule, but I need my beauty sleep, and those two fight all the time." Buzz raised her voice as she ended her sentence so the sisters in the kitchen could hear.

"Okay, I guess," Mabel said, but she had already decided where she was going be sleeping from now on.

Following the redhead into the kitchen, she saw that Emma was already up and reading at the table, or at least pretending to as she listened to everything happening. The teen always rolled her eyes and said she hated breakfast, but she didn't miss it either.

"Maby! Didn't think we'd see you this morning," Lucy said, but her eyes were on Cliff and their joined hands. Her expression said nothing about whether she was happy or not about it, which meant she was okay with it. Happiness would come in time.

Harper looked up from cutting carrots and gave a similar glance at Cliff and their hands. Shaking her head, she said, "Sloppy seconds, Mabs?"

"Grow up, Harper. They're in love." Lucy shoved her sister hard, making Harper's hand brush the already cut carrots, sending them flying across the kitchen onto the floor.

"Lucy! Now I have to start over." Harper pushed her back.

"Just pick them up and wash them!" Lucy stated, pushing Harper again.

"Nobody pays for floor carrots, Luce." Harper pushed her again.

"Stop fighting!" Sera yelled from behind Cliff and Mabel. "How can I get married and move away if you kids are constantly fighting? Who will break it up when I'm not here? Nobody, that's who."

"Maybe they'll stop when they are adults," Emma said sarcastically from the table.

Without missing a beat, Harper picked up the last of the carrots on her cutting board and threw them at the dark-haired teenager. Many of them hit the kid, forcing her to give her oldest sister a dirty look, which was returned by Harper sticking her tongue out at her.

"Cliff, did you stay here last night?" Sera demanded as she always did. Not that it ever mattered who stayed overnight, except Cliff was the only one who was a constant in the house.

"No, Mom Lovely, I did not. We just got here." He smiled at her. Today he was in slacks and a dress shirt to impress her. Since everyone else was either still in pajamas or in jeans and a T-shirt, Cliff had assured Mabel that it would work. But based on her expression, it wasn't.

"We?" she asked and then noticed the hands, which Mabel tried to drop like a hot potato, but Cliff held on tight. Apparently, there was no getting out of this one. Not that Sera shouldn't have guessed this might happen since she knew that they had been sleeping together. Well, more than sleeping together.

"We." He pulled Mabel into his arms and kissed her forehead.

Staking his claim, more likely, but she let him. She was his.

Sera looked at them, then at Lucy and back. "So now you are going to be in Maby's room and not Lucy's every morning? Will you be paying rent? The water bill?"

"Our plan is for Maby to move in with me since I'm closer to the U anyway." Which was his logic last night for her to move in. That and so they could have sex anytime without a sister walking in. The second reason had been why she had agreed to it.

"YES!" Buzz yelled from across the room as she did a small victory dance.

"Not until she's married," Sera stated, putting her hand up to stop Buzz's excitement as her eyes locked on Cliff's. She was making up rules as she went. In fact, Sera had never thought in terms of marriage until she got engaged. Now it was all she thought about.

"Then we'll get married." Cliff held Sera's gaze.

"Don't get married just to shack up." Sera folded her arms, not breaking the eye contact.

"I'm marrying her because I am madly and deeply in love with her. Because I can't see my life without her in it, the center of it. And of course, to make you happy," he said.

"Why her and not the other one?" Sera asked, indicating at Lucy.

"I don't know, but Maby is the one that I'm madly in love with. In fact, I think we'll be getting married in three weeks from yesterday."

"Impossible," Sera scoffed. "Weddings take time."

"We're getting married in Florida, on the beach." This, they hadn't discussed, but it seemed they didn't have to because it sounded exactly like what she wanted. It was exactly how she wanted to marry Cliff, where they had fallen in love.

"No, I'll plan it." Sera waved off Cliff's idea, instantly taking over. "So, once you're married, how are you going to support my Mabel Lucie?"

"Sera!" Mabel didn't need the man she loved to prove how he would be taking care of her, as if she couldn't take care of herself.

Cliff didn't seem to notice Mabel's anger at the question as he answered, "My new job comes with a nice salary. She'll never want for anything."

"New job?" Lucy asked in surprise.

"Director of Philanthropy at Scott Industries."

"Sounds made up." Harper pointed a knife at him, since she had started cutting carrots again.

"Scott Industries? As in, funded the library, Scott Industries? As in funding the new gymnasium at the U, Scott Industries? As in Clifton Scott IV of Scott Industries!" Buzz stared at him. "Clifton Scott V? VI?"

"Just the fifth. Maybe one day Maby will carry the sixth."

"Holy fuck!" Buzz sat down, missing the stool and landing on her ass. "Maby will be loaded."

"I don't care about the money, Buzzy," Mabel stated, hoping nobody thought she was marrying him for money.

"You have money? I'm making you a bill for all the stuff you have sponged off me in the last year. I think it's thousands? Millions?" Sera spun around and headed to the living room, looking for paper to create her bill.

"I'm getting champagne. We need to celebrate." Harper stopped chopping and headed for the basement as Agatha came in the room.

Her eyes were blurry, and she was carrying Violet, who was still in her pajamas, her head was resting on her shoulder. The woman was already in sweats and an oversized green Grand Cannon T-shirt. "Why can't family drama happen at a decent hour?"

"Maby and Cliff are getting married!" Lucy said in excitement. More excitement than Mabel had expected this morning.

"Your Cliff?" Agatha asked her in confusion.

"He was never mine," Lucy stated, as if she didn't usually call him "My Cliff."

"Congrats, Maby. Hopefully, he doesn't move in, and you're happy with him." Agatha put the little girl on her feet, who ran to Buzz, who was back on a stool but not sitting straight. She must have hit her ass hard.

"Actually, I'm moving in with him," she replied, though she didn't want to move away from her family. She knew how Sera felt.

"I hope you do better at moving than Mom has. We might have to use a crowbar to get her to leave." Agatha grabbed a carrot chunk and ate it.

"I am moving out one day. By the time the wedding happens, I'll be gone." Sera had a piece of paper and a pen now and was starting to write things down. Violet settled on her lap.

Harper burst up the stairs. "So I have two kinds of champagne, one left over from the engagement party Buzz killed last month and one from the wedding we did last summer. It was a success, but I think they're getting a divorce. Now, that's not the champagne's fault; it's the couple's fault. Keep that in mind." She grabbed the bottle opener and started opening the first bottle.

"Cursed champagne, Harper. That won't keep them together," Buzz stated as she went for glasses, not ones for wine, but regular water glasses.

With a pop, the first bottle started bubbling over and down to the countertop and the floor. Harper started opening the other one.

Lucy grabbed the open bottle before Buzz could and tossed it into the sink behind her with a loud crash of broken glass. "No need for champagne, everyone. Let's just do orange juice."

"Mimosas," Harper said with excitement as the second bottle

popped and started bubbling and spilling. It made Mabel realized that Harper always asked others to open the bubbly at functions. Her sister clearly couldn't do it without spilling.

"No, Harper. We don't need alcohol to have a good time." Lucy grabbed the bottle and tossed it into the sink with the other one. The second didn't break.

"Who says?" Buzz hurried around the counter to save some of the champagne.

"I did. We, as a family, drink too much," Lucy stated, her eyes on Mabel.

"Lucy, no, champagne is fine. It's a celebration after all," Mabel said, staring at her sister, telling her to leave it alone.

"Not fine." Lucy folded her arms.

"Don't. Or else."

"You don't, and …"

Cliff whispered something into her ear, but she wasn't listening to him as she stared her twin down. Today was not the day to address anything that they had talked about the night before.

"Maby has a drinking problem," Lucy shouted out.

"Lucy is dyslexic," Mabel responded.

"What?" Sera stopped and looked at both of them.

"Nothing," they both said at the same time.

"No. Don't 'nothing' me. What are you, ten? These are both serious issues, you two. Both of you sit down." Sera pointed at the table. It had been years since they were forced to sit and talk about something. Mostly because as kids, it never worked.

Letting Cliff go, Mabel sat down next to Agatha, who got up and moved away from the table. She didn't want to be caught in the middle of whatever was coming.

"Let's go by birth order. Mabel Lucie, a drinking problem? You don't drink." Sera sat down across from them and pointed out.

"I had a little bit of an issue with it in college. I don't drink much anymore. I have it under control." There, that was easy. Why had she even been dreading this?

"She almost died, Mom," Lucy squealed on her.

"Died?! That is *not* a little problem." Sera's eyes were locked on hers as tears ran down her cheeks. Sera never could control her emotions. Mabel usually didn't think much about that night because it had happened so long ago.

"Lucy can't read!" If Lucy could do it, she could.

"Still on you, Mabel. Talk," Sera stated.

Mabel looked around the room. All eyes were on her. Even Lucy was staring at her, but under the table, her twin took her hand in hers, holding it tight in support. Closing her eyes because she couldn't look at her family and speak, she said, "I went into an alcohol-induced coma in college. It was caused by binge drinking while on speed. I was saved by a freshman who did CPR on me until the ambulance came. I got lucky. Next time, maybe not so. So, I try and stay away from drinking a lot."

"Where was I? I was supposed to be called for shit like that!" Sera slammed her hand into the table, her anger palpable.

"They called Dad, but he didn't come." Mabel shrugged, and Lucy squeezed her hand. They all tried to not let their birth parents' rejection of them hurt, but it did.

"From here on out, I am everyone's emergency contact, married or not. I am number one on that list." Sera looked around the room as if someone was going to tell her no.

"You married or me married?" Buzz asked for clarification, the reporter side of her coming out as she ate a cinnamon roll.

"It doesn't matter, Beatrix!" Sera hissed at her, stopping any further questions.

"Why didn't you ever tell us?" Harper asked, sitting down at the table next to Sera.

"I didn't want to be treated different, and I still don't. I can control it, but I don't want it pushed in my face all the time." Mabel's free hand was tapping the table, mimicking Lucy, except hers was because she hated being the center of attention. And right now, all the attention was on her.

"Nobody would do that." Harper took her hand and squeezed it, making the tapping stop. "Okay, we won't do that anymore."

"We will all try harder to not be so much into alcohol. We are adults, so we should be able to not have it around all the time. Right, everyone?" Sera promised, and everyone behind her either agreed or nodded. Then she turned her attention to Mabel's twin. "Now, dyslexia?"

"It's nothing. It has never almost killed me, and I don't actually have it. It's something Cliff made up," Lucy argued and glared at Cliff.

Harper got up and went back into the kitchen to start chopping carrots again, but after two, she stopped and pulled out her phone.

"Dyslexia is a learning disorder involving reading, writing, and spelling," Mabel told the group as she continued to hold Lucy's hand despite her twin trying to get away.

"See, I don't have it. I can read and write, and I am a damn good speller!" Lucy finally got her hand away from Mabel and held both up in victory.

"Spell yellow," Cliff asked from his stool. He was watching Harper on her phone and was wearing her Yelling Stan T-shirt. All the words were spelled wrong. In fact, over half the people in the room were wearing a shirt with something spelled wrong on it. All made by Lucy.

"I don't have to spell things to prove I can. This isn't school, and I'm an adult," Lucy argued with her friend. "In fact, I'm still pissed at you for sleeping with Maby."

"No, you're not because you stopped calling it fucking," Cliff pointed out.

"Is Mom or Agatha wearing a Grand Cannon T-shirt?" Harper asked, not looking at her sister, just looking at her phone. Reading.

Lucy looked from her mom to Agatha and grinned. "Agatha is."

"They both are, Lucy," Mabel informed her quietly.

Lucy got up and pushed away from everyone. "You know what? I don't care. So I'm not as smart as everyone else. I'm actually still a great person. Not everyone needs a college education; I am doing just fine as it is."

"Lucy, don't be mad." Sera started to get up.

"Why not, Sera? You all think I'm stupid. Why not think I'm

disabled also?" She rushed past before anyone could stop her and ran up the stairs.

"Cliff is right. That is what she has." Harper looked up from her phone. "It's all here."

"I know," Mabel agreed, "but we all have to be better for her. No more making fun of her, and we have to help her whenever we can."

"But only if she lets you," Cliff said, sitting down next to Mabel at the table. "It's not something we can force on her. It has to be her decision."

"What if she never decides to get help?" Harper asked.

"Then she makes her own way, without help."

"Maybe we just need to push her. I mean, push her toward asking for help." Harper picked up her knife but didn't start cutting again.

"Lucy doesn't work that way," Mabel said.

"Maby is right; just let her be. One day she will realize that she wants help. We will be ready then. But until then, we do everything we can to make her life easier," Sera said and got to her feet. "Anyone else have a condition you want to tell me about?"

The rest of the sisters shook their heads in denial. Nobody wanted a lecture today.

"Well, with that excitement, I'm heading to bed. Don't wake me for anything," Agatha stated and left the room, and everyone stared after her until she vanished up the stairs.

"Well, that was rude," Buzz said to the room quietly.

"So, Sera, are you letting Maby get married before you? It's suddenly a race to the altar," Harper commented while dicing more carrots. It seemed she was getting nowhere on her dicing this morning.

"When you know, Harper, you know. One day, it'll be you."

"Not a chance, and if I ever get married, it will be because he's a billionaire who swoons at my feet."

"And lets you boss him around," Emma stated with a chuckle.

"You think that should hurt, but it doesn't. A man has to know his place. Isn't that right, Cliff?" She pointed the knife at him.

"Yes, Harper. As always, you are right," Cliff answered with a grin.

"You know, once you get married to her, you'll be family, which means the gloves will be off. I will beat you when you need it."

"I would like to see you try." Cliff sat down next to Mabel and put his arms around her.

"I'll give you to the count of three, just because we're not related yet," Harper said, setting down her knife again and scooping up the carrots and putting them in a bowl calmly. "One."

"You can scare your sisters, and you can scare those losers you date, but you do not scare me, Harper Lovely," Cliff stated, his arm still around Mabel, but she shook him off. He didn't know who he was up against, but Mabel did. Harper could be mean if she wanted to be, and she usually wanted to be.

"Two," Harper continued, and Mabel started for the living room. Maybe the love of her life wasn't as smart as he seemed.

"I am not—" He stopped talking because Harper was on the move.

Cliff picked up Mabel on his way past, causing her to scream-laugh as he carried her through the house, up the stairs, and down the hallway into her bedroom, Harper fast on his heels the entire trip. Luckily, her knife was gone.

Cliff slammed the door and dropped Mabel to her feet before slamming the lock shut. He was breathing heavily and staring at the door.

"Ballsy, aren't you?" Mabel teased and walked over to him, boxing him in against the door.

"Brave as hell," he panted out, his eyes looking at the door.

"I thought you knew better than to underestimate Harper. What were you doing in this house for over a year?"

"You already know I wasn't doing the right thing, because I should have been getting to know you. I missed a year with you, and you were right here. So close." He spun them so that she was against the door, and his hands were holding hers above her head.

"I'll never let it happen again. I'm not letting you go again."

"Good."

EPILOGUE

A MONTH later

"MABY, WAKE UP." Cliff shook her, and as predicted, she growled at him. It wasn't the first time he had woken her up in the middle of the night. Mostly it had been for sex, but not this time. "Maby, wake up," Cliff tried again.

"Cliff, just wait for morning. Then I'll rock your world," her husky voice said. Mabel didn't open her eyes as she rolled onto her back. The sheet slipped, exposing her right breast.

"Not that, Lovely," he said but couldn't not kiss the nipple that instantly pebbled under his lips and tongue. After nearly a month, her body still instantly responded to his touch, which caused his own to react just as quickly.

"Seems like that. Now I swear I'll blow your world in the a.m. It's my wedding night. I need sleep." But she arched her back as he continued kissing her breast.

"*Tomorrow* is your wedding night. Tonight is your pre-wedding night." He shifted, painfully hard in his sweats from just looking at her exposed body and listening to her husky promises.

"I still need sleep for that. This might be why Sera didn't want me to stay here tonight. Something about bad luck and tradition and you waking me in the middle of the night for sex, so I don't get a good night's sleep," she moaned. "The other one needs attention. You know how jealous they get."

Chucking, he pulled the sheet down. Her deep concern that one breast was getting more attention than the other was cute. It made him wonder if it was a neglected twin thing. Or if she just liked him paying attention to her breasts and didn't want to say it. Except she was more than willing to say anything else about their sex life.

Once done with that breast, he sat up. "Now that you're awake, we need to talk."

One brown eye popped open and looked at him. "Why? Or, more importantly, why did you get me all excited for sex and then want to talk? Such a chick move."

"Can we talk?" he asked seriously, or as seriously as he could because she was grinning, and he loved her little grins.

"Go ahead." She slipped her hands behind her head, a move that intentionally thrust her breasts at him.

"I wanted to ask you to marry me." He ran a hand over her flat stomach.

"You did not seriously wake me to ask me to marry you. I'm marrying you in like twelve hours. Sera and your parents invited the entire town. I feel you should remember that."

"I mean right now."

"Like we're kids and do a blood oath? Isn't in front of the entire town enough for you?"

"Like I have a judge in the living room willing to marry us. I just need you to invite anyone you want to be here."

Instantly, she pulled the sheet over her naked body, a blush running up her chest and face. "You do not."

"I do. Call your sisters and let me marry you just like we wanted, minus the beach, the sun, and the ocean. Us, your family, and no crowds. No big dresses, and no Scotts around."

"But what about the wedding? The one later?"

"We do that one for everyone else. But we do one tonight for us."

"Sera will kill us."

"Don't invite her; just your sister's. Sera will enjoy the big wedding she planned tomorrow way more." Cliff said, knowing that Sera would probably stop a wedding that didn't involve doves at this point. Best for her not to be there.

"Yes," she whispered without hesitation. "What do I wear?"

"Whatever you want. I was thinking this." He waved his hands over her naked body.

"I can't get married naked! I'll call them once I get dressed."

"Make it quick. The judge isn't exactly happy with me, but he owes my dad, so he'll be here."

Leaving her behind to get dressed and call her sisters, Cliff went to sit with the judge in the living room, who wasn't up for conversation. He was more than willing to take a beer, though, which was the only liquor in the house, and it was only there for when her sisters came. Lucy still enjoyed a beer, arguing that if Mabel could read, she could drink. It was only fair.

Whatever Mabel said got the sisters from the Lovely house to their apartment in a record eleven minutes. It was usually a twenty-minute drive on a good traffic day. By that time, Mabel had changed into pajama pants and a white tank top, which was too sexy for company, but it was only her sisters, so it didn't matter.

Lucy was the first in the door and pushed him against the wall before calling to Mabel, "Get your things, and let's go!"

Harper took over and pushed his chest, holding him against the wall. He had no idea what Mabel had said to them, but it was about him, and it was bad.

"I left the car right outside the door, and the engine is running," Buzz stated from behind her.

"You should have shut it off. It might get towed. What were you thinking?" Harper turned on her sister, letting Cliff go in the process.

"That Maby needed us, and there wasn't time to do much once we got here," Buzz stated, not backing down.

"Who's the dude?" Agatha asked, the only one not in pajamas but still in the clothes from the day before.

"Judge Ramper. Are these the witnesses finally?" He got to his feet, tired of waiting.

"Yes, they are," Cliff said, even as Harper shoved him one more time into the wall.

"What are we witnessing?" Lucy demanded.

"Our wedding," Cliff said. He really needed Harper to stop pushing him into the wall.

"That's in hours. You woke me for that? I need my sleep, Maby!" Buzz complained.

"The wedding is now. So, all of you sit on the couch." Mabel took charge. Agatha slammed the door and claimed the wing chair, not wanting to squish on the couch with her three sisters.

The others followed, sitting on the couch, watching, and not saying anything. Cliff took Mabel's hand and kissed it before going to where the judge pointed. Within minutes he pronounced them husband and wife and signed the paperwork.

Harper demanded she be able to sign as a witness, joined by Lucy because she was Mabel's twin and best friend. Lucy had argued that she should be able to sign the certificate two times just for that.

With everything signed and done, the judge left, and Maby kicked her sisters out, all of them complaining that they had come down there for only a few minutes.

Once the door was closed, he smiled at his bride. "Exactly how I wanted to do it."

"Exactly?"

"I wanted more sand, but I get to trade that for having sex with my new wife minutes after marrying her. Time is priceless."

"You think you're getting sex? Now that we are married, we don't have to do that except on anniversaries and birthdays." Her words weren't even out of her mouth before he was carrying her to bed to show her how he felt about ending their sex life.

After dropping her on the bed, he instantly pulled her pants off and crawled up after her. "You like sex just as much as I do, Mrs. Scott."

"Say that again."

"You like sex as much as I do."

"No, the other."

"Mrs. Scott.

"Cliff, are we really married?"

"Forever, Mabel Lucie Scott."

"Thank you."

"For what?"

"For letting me trick you into that trip to Florida. For falling in love with me."

"It was the best trip I have ever taken."

"Me too."

The End

The series continues with Harper Lovely, who has her bossiness challenged by her actual boss Kaine Hawthorn in Falling for the Boss.

Visit my web page for more information WWW.ALIEGARNETT.COM

BONUS SCENE: MABEL & HARPER IN THE GROG'S RESTROOM.

Harper's vise-like grip didn't let up until they were in the two-stall bathroom. Everyone agreed that the stall by the wall was the good one. The other was a crapshoot, something you didn't want in a public toilet.

Since the good stall was occupied, Harper said nothing, just stared at her, scowling.

The occupant must have taken too long for Harper because she pounded on the door and yelled, "Be done, or you will regret it."

Instantly, the toilet flushed, and a woman barely old enough to be legal came out of the stall, looking at them with more than a little fear. She turned on the water tap, only to have Harper stomp over and shut it off.

"Did you pee on your hands?" Harper hissed.

"N-n-no," the girl stammered.

"Then you don't need to wash them." She pushed the woman out the door.

Then she locked it and turned to Mabel, looked her up and down, and shook her head. "What the hell, Mabel Lucie Atwell Lovely? Cliff. *Lucy's* Cliff. Is the world out of men, so you had to bang him?"

"Uhm," she started.

"Cliff, Mabel Lucie Atwell? What do you even see in him? *Is* there something to see in him?" Harper folded her arms and looked up at the dirty stained ceiling. "Does Lucy know?"

Before she could answer, Harper went on. "Of course, she doesn't know. She's with you two, while you guys make eyes at each other. Eyes, Mabel Lucy Atwell Lovely, eyes! Do you think you can hide from her forever?"

"I ..." she tried but was interrupted by a pounding on the door.

"Of course you can't. And by the time you get tired of screwing around behind your sister's back, it will be too late. She'll find out and then what happens? Do you know what will happen?"

"N—" The pounding came again, but Harper ignored it.

"Nobody does. Because when Lucy gets mad, she gets super mad. She has two emotions, Mabel Lucie Atwell." Harper didn't finish because someone pounded again on the locked door. Calmly, she turned from Mabel and opened the door, sticking her head out. "Find somewhere else to piss, lady. I'm in here lecturing. So, unless you want in on this, leave."

Slamming the door shut, she locked it again. "Now, where was I?" She shut her eyes and shook her head for a bit, mumbling to herself. Then snapped back at Mabel, "What the hell, Mabel Lucie Atwell Lovely!"

"I—"

"Sleeping with Cliff is crossing a line. It was invisible, but everyone else saw it. I saw it, not that I ever thought of sleeping with him. I mean, gross, it's Cliff. Was it as gross as I thought it would be?"

This time she didn't answer, which pissed Harper off even more. "I know it was. Now I want you to stay in here for a few hours and think about what you've done. You've done some bad stuff in your time, but this is the worst by far. Except that time you almost eloped, and I had to stop it."

Frowning at Harper, Maby wanted to tell her that that wasn't her, but she knew her sister wasn't done. Her sister was never done.

"That might not have been you, but this tops that one. Cliff!" she yelled and shook her fists at the ceiling, then walked out of the bathroom.

Mabel leaned against the wall and tried to breathe. Everything Harper had said was true, except for the gross part because not once had it been gross with Cliff.

But if Harper couldn't understand, Lucy never would, which meant there was no way she was telling her.

The End

ABOUT THE AUTHOR

I love to read and prefer a little spice in those books. I am lucky enough to live on a small hobby farm in northern Minnesota with her husband and two kids. I enjoy spending time in the pasture with my two mini horses and one fainting goat (who doesn't actually faint). When I'm not writing, I'm busy trying to do all the things I didn't get to while writing. Or maybe I wouldn't have gotten to them anyway, because its laundry, dishes and fun things like that.

ALSO BY ALIE GARNETT

<u>Indulge</u>

Craving Winter

Enticing Aurora

<u>Landstad, ND</u>

Invisible

Irresistible

Impulsive

Insuppressible

Intriguing

Imperfect

Irreplaceable

<u>The Great Lovely Falls</u>

Falling for the Single Mom

Falling for his Best Friends Sister

Falling for the Boss

Falling for his Step-Sister

Falling for his Fake Wife

Falling into a Second Chance

<u>Hart Series</u>

Seeing her Pain

Her Favor

Max Valentine is Looking at Me!

Keeping her Safe

<u>Stand Alone</u>

Romancing the Doctor